PODS OF BUBBLEDUMB

A STUDY IN MASS DEPRAVITY

BY

JIM OWENS

Copyright © *Jim Owens*,.2024

All Rights Reserved

This book is subject to the condition that no part of this book is to be reproduced, transmitted in any form or means; electronic or mechanical, stored in a retrieval system, photocopied, recorded, scanned, or otherwise. Any of these actions require the proper written permission of the author.

Table of Contents

PLASTIC GODS 1
TIGHTEN THE SPHINCTERS! 9
TUG OF WAR 16
THE TWO MELS 22
DINK NOOKY 38
AN EVENING WITH GHANT 60
THE REVELATION 65
RED MAWA CAPS 69
CELLPHONE DISENGAGEMENT 72
FRONTIER CONFEDERATES 75
A SAVAGE BLOW 80
PENNY FOR A PAUPER 83
LGBTQ IN THE PARK 86
FLIGHT OF THE PHOENIX 92
THE GHANT RANT 99
TUG THE REPUG 104
GIBBY 107
DIGGING FOR TRUTH 109
OLIVER ON A ROLL 112
GIVING TUG A JUMP 119
THE RUPTURE 122
HAIL THE MIGHTY CHIEF, MAY HE WALK IN THE LORD'S FOOTSTEPS 127
HIS MAJESTY'S BRIBE 130
A LOOK TOWARD CANADA 132

THE MAGIC TAPESTRY	137
ALL BY HIMSELF	140
ERUPTION!	142
SNOBBY BOBBY	144
LISA GROWS ILL	147
EARTHLY DEMISE OF A SPIRITED ALTRUIST	151
WORN AND WILTED	154
WITHERED TITTIES	159
HIGH CRIMES AND A GREAT BIG YAWN	162
KABOOM!	164
JASMINE	167
SQUEEZING OUT THE LITTLE GUY	169
DISGUSTED COHORTS	171
THE SAVIOR	174
A DATE FOR MELANIE	181
NINE DREAMS	184
THE I-55 EYEBALL EXCAVATOR	191
OLIVER STUMBLES	195
SPARKY'S PARADISE INN	198
RIOTS ON MAIN STREET	202
TWO DICKS IN SUITS	206
SHABBY TABBY	210
BOTH FEET IN	214
SADIE COMES TO PLAY (SERIAL KILLER MEETS SERIAL KILLER)	217
MINACIOUS PROPOSALS	221
IN A SNAP	224

UN-RAPPING THINE EVIL	232
RENDEZVOUS	240
AFTERMATH	246
ACCOLADES	250
TURBULENT WATERS	252
THREE WEEKS LATER	254
WINTER BARRELS IN	259
THREE YEARS LATER BONKERS!	262
THE DEMISE OF JOY MCRAE	265
APPENDIX A	269
APPENDIX B	271
APPENDIX C	273
APPENDIX D	276
APPENDIX E	280
APPENDIX F	281

PLASTIC GODS

At the inception of time, which, of course, no one knows when and if it actually occurred, God created humans, it is said. At first, nobody thought to ask "Who or what created God?" God just appeared and then whipped up the universe. This God guy just sort of hung out there in the sparkling heavens, waiting to invent the first "intelligent" being. And when God did, it was a glorious but lonely individual known as man.

Oh, and then God created woman—that glorious creature who would stand by man and make him greater. Was woman a mere afterthought? Was she destined to toil endless hours as a servant to man? Was she to be content with second place in the Universe for the rest of time?

No. She was not. But from the warped whims of this early male creature sprang the fallacious idea that because man was physically bigger and stronger than woman, so too, man must be mentally and emotionally superior. Thus, was born the flawed philosophy that woman would have to tend to and follow man for eternity. Moreover, God was considered a male. Never mind the future, confidence-building tales of societies where women ruled, the crux of most religious philosophy was that God must be a male, and the male spirit would forever dominate. That was the intention of male religion inventors, at least.

Most of the female offspring of the first man and woman went along with this theory. However, with a few--just a handful, mind you--the crazy notion failed to stimulate their thinking, and so, a nucleus of female resistance planted itself, germinated and carried on quietly through the doleful ages until that magic day when they would rise up and take their place as equals to any self-proclaimed stronger being.

Meanwhile, religion began to develop to explain the making of the universe by God. Of course, the Thronez, one of the oldest of the modern religions, were the progenitors of the flawed logic behind man's creation and rule. And the older the religion, the more time it had to embellish old tales and spin new stories. Soon, the various religions competed against each other for followers. The religion marketplace swarmed with salespeople in the form of faith peddlers.

Finally, the offspring of the offspring yielded a man named Gore Binger. Gore was a Thronez. Some of God's men (the Thronez) tortured Gore to death for suggesting that perhaps war was unnecessary and that God could possess characteristics of both the female and male species. Other of God's men (the Gorebingers) twisted and squeezed this poor soul into a showcase for their salvation and wove from his sufferings their Holy Gospel. Gore, a peaceful man who was intellectually ahead of the rest of humanity by eons, was tied to a type of "Z"-frame made of wood, starved, burnt, and cut up into tiny pieces "for daring to promulgate the idea that God could be a Hermaphrodite," a supreme entity with both manly and womanly features. So, the putrefaction of Gore Binger's brain, it was thought, needed to be burned out of human existence. Even the Thronez women lined up to hurl fruit at the hapless, hermaphrodite-hyping heretic before he met his gruesome death. Gore Binger cried, "No. No. I am not saying that God is a hermaphrodite. God has no sex organs. I'm just saying he has, to better understand both sexes, intangible attributes of both woman and man." But the male dominated Thronez did not care to hear his explanation, and so the strange man perished among the crackling flames.

Since Gore's outrageous and audacious claim of a double-sex God sparked the fight in man, his name became synonymous with "war," and two great wars were named for him: World Gore I and World Gore II. So, on crept mankind, while competitors with the Thronez and Gorebingerz religions materialized. There were the Muzzles and the Weirdoz, for instance." And then there were the different factions of the Gorebingerz, each having its own twist on Gore Binger and his supposed future return to earth. From these groups there were the Spongez, a wealthy super-conservative faction who believed in end-times and The Rapture; the Southern Badpests, a hillbilly pack of Gorebingerz; the Allcons, a recent and arrogant lot of petty thieves and polygamists who had been tossed out of several States in their brief history; and the Cathartics, a faction replete with odd hats and bizarre ceremonies. These Gorebingerz,, to make up for the human cruelty that exterminated Gore, tagged him as "The Son of God" and the vessel for mankind's salvation.

Now for every good, there must be an evil. And so, for every God there must be an evil being. The Gorebingers call this evil being "The Devil." Again, this being is a male. It is not that The Devil wanted to be a male, but they made him one. Anything bad that happened could, from then on, be blamed on The Devil. And because they burned and chopped up Gore Binger for lending God what they thought were tangible attributes of both sexes, they expanded on their description of The Devil by lending him red skin, horns and a pointed tail. Oh, and a pitchfork, perhaps to satisfy the hillbilly farmers of the Southern Badpests.

The closest one of God's beings ever came to mirroring The Devil, in modern times, was one Heinrich Schroeder. He exterminated scores upon scores of Thronez. But throughout the ages many other beings vied for the position of most reviled evildoer, such as Genghis Khan, Napoleon Bonaparte and Attila the Hun. Oddly, all of these low-life barbarians would eventually find their way onto the list known as "The Greatest Conquerors," as if acts of wholesale torture, slaughter and destruction were a grand gift to humanity. Both man and woman celebrated the conquerors' genocidal ingenuity.

Now we arrive at one of the subjects of this modern-day depiction of evil, in the name of Douglas "Tug" McRae, a relatively small-time slaughterer in what is known as The Prairie State, even though there yet exists very little prairie of which we can speak or write. Illinois, they officially named it. Tug, the "Great," might we say, made his home in Illinois. How woman and feline extinguish this regional conqueror, we shall reveal.

Our story also features Oliver Rhodes, the neo-hippie and relentless institution stomper; Elma Ray, a most lovely heroine of color; and the Goodalls, Melanie and Melvin, a pair of greedy, affluent, fanatical, hypocritical Gorebingerz of the Spongez variety.

Here, it must be stated, that most consumers of religion, as individuals, have good intentions and perform good deeds. As groups, though, religious institutions tend to gravitate toward harnessing their group power and influencing politics, thus embarking on the idea to force-feed their morals and values to the rest of society. And large religious organizations adversely affect the population in other ways. For example, religion lulled the world into sleeping through horrendous wars, or Gores, giving impetus to the erroneous notion that bloody battles among the planet's denizens were inevitable. So, wars waged throughout the ages are revisited as subjects of hard study during the school and church sessions of our youth.

Let us jump to the eighteenth century and the founding of America, where all the religions were encouraged to practice their faith, even though they continually tried to get around the separation of church and state as best they could. The good religious people kept their noses out of government; but the bad religious people found a way to meddle with and influence the government of the United States of America.

With all of the various religions gathering every Sunday to collect cash in exchange for hope and reassurance, the human mind began to obsess on righteous and saintly behaviors. So obsessed became many, that their judgment grew warped. This curious process advanced until copious cuckoos contaminated the population, and the shallow fools began wandering about the crooked streets with intentions to monitor and control every other living thing. And those who could see right through the sky-bound-soul-for-money exchanging in these untaxed houses of worship, also had to deal with the steel-cold fact that, since they harbored no false hope and no arrogant fantasy that stems from thinking that one is worthy of some forever paradise upon death, they also had to exist with zero faith. Now, knowing that you will perish and that nothing else will become of you, wears on the human brain as well, so a number of these so-called atheists grew cuckoo and wandered the same crooked streets as the delusional do-gooders. That makes for a lot of cuckoos. So, they took their places right next to the Gore-Binger-obsessed cuckoos, the self-appointed "select" ones of the Thronez,, and the rest of the earthly beasts who roamed the planet. The atheist cuckoos were racked by reality, and the whole world swam with them, waltzed with them, and bore their downhearted presence.

Meanwhile, capitalism and the corporation boomed in young America, and the business of unprecedented growth brought new and more complicated products into the fold, and maximized the stresses of a dog-eat-dog society until a blade-happy public gave way to a gun-happy public where, you guessed it, even more cuckoos emerged. Then, the new Information Age let everyone know that, no, the Civil War had not solved the issue of human worth and placement in our society and, yes, resentment still boiled in the background like wicked broth in a witch's cauldron. Thus, in this Information Age, the cuckoo became so common that being cuckoo grew into the new norm. And they all carried guns!

In the second decade of the 21st century there came trotting up to the podium one Oscar K. Schmidt, a reprehensible extremist candidate who could make claim to every bad behavior known to woman or man. Schmidt turned the world upside-down, making lies the norm, and truth, the outrageous. The

Conservapricks elected him, the Librhoids cringed, and America changed forever, becoming the joke of the universe. Thankfully, the people unelected him four years later, although, on January 6, 2021, there was an insurrection at the Capitol as a result of the Schmidt followers' discontent.

Schmidt made for a formidable scalawag and almost brought the country to its knees, but he just lacked the mental capacity to transform his full-scale, totalitarian dream into reality. He possessed an enormous capability to hoodwink the public and introduce boundless confusion into society and politics, but he could not manage to deconstruct the silos which isolated the various hate groups and militias he needed in order for him to seize total control. Nor could Schmidt extricate himself from his self-induced snafus, and he suffered for it at the next election. Thus, his progress of converting America into a dictatorship, where he would wield all power, was arrested by his own blockheadedness and an innate ability to make bad worse. He inherited mountains of dollars but lacked the sense to usurp the authority he craved. Though mounds of damage followed his election, he just did not have the wherewithal to complete what he had started.

Unfortunately, the American electorate, having had enough of another weak liberal President, who served after Schmidt, brought in a new, bolder, aspiring tyrant with even less morals and more mouth than his conservative predecessor. The Librhoid Party was stunned. Just when no one thought a more repulsive human figure could possibly supplant Schmidt, there he appeared. And the fallout from all of this lunacy, on a national, state and local level, is a story to be told.

The lame American public got hornswoggled by this fraudster, this flimflammer. America just laid right down and took it up the wazoo. At first, nobody did anything about the outlandish leadership that ensued, but the casualties began to stack up so incredibly high that the option of doing nothing fell obsolete. That the government will have to step in and rescue humankind from its own folly became more apparent as the days passed by.

Ghant Wackersham, the new president, created a polarized relationship with the public: people either adored him or despised him. Deception, Wackersham's only true ally, would also be his downfall.

Fast forward to the year 2028, during the reign of Lord Gore, and a bizarre tale unfolds of woman vs. man leading up to another, even worse, insurrection. In this event, both political and religious fanatics believed they knew what was best for humanity and did their utmost to impose their twisted plans on everyone else.

This, then, is a story of courageous women and universal madmen.

TIGHTEN THE SPHINCTERS!

The lively waitresses at Ray's Roundup Restaurant hurried past a group of young students. Carrying coffee pots and large circular trays of food, they weaved between tables like pinballs. The dim lighting barely illuminated several cheap paintings of lasso-wielding cowboys chasing broncos and big-wheeled pickup trucks splashing through mudholes. Near the checkout counter, a photo of Grandfather Ray's original neon sign evoked a more innocent era when teenagers and young college students with saddle shoes and pompadour hairstyles sipped malted milks at long wooden counters. But now, in 2028, patrons drank coffee and energy drinks, arrived with smartphones and laptops, and mostly kept to themselves, huddled in dark corners, communicating primarily through the internet. At other tables voices buzzed, as mainstream rock music droned in the background of the cozy establishment on Grand Avenue in the State Capitol of Springfield, Illinois, just south of Runyon's Hamburgers with its ubiquitous blue triangular-arched logo.

Finally, a waitress brought the receipts and asked if there was anything else the patrons needed. As she gathered the plates and cups, a burst of laughter from the front briefly drowned out the music and drew everyone's attention. "Hmmm. I wonder what they're smokin'?" the skinny, middle-aged waitress joked before disappearing into the crowd with an armload of dirty dishes. Despite knowing that the money-tight college crowd usually left minimal tips, she remained friendly and amicable. Then, just as the soporific rock ballads had about drained the place of anymore life, the sharp sound of a plate breaking on the ceramic kitchen floor brought a cheer from the excitement-starved college students. Meanwhile, four students at the small, square, white-with-gold speckled table griped and moaned about their financial woes.

"My school books were so expensive that I had to get my mom to help pay for them," remarked Martha Graves as she took the last bite of her Vegan Platter, a Ray's Specialty. Martha, a 20-year-old Gorebinger and psychology major at Heart of Illinois College, dreamed of treating patients in an assembly-line fashion, just as doctors do today.

"Yeah, I had to use my credit card," added Randy Roswell. "I'm not even halfway to graduation and I'm already in a ton of debt." He crumpled his napkin and tossed it into his empty soup bowl, which a busboy quickly scooped up. Randy, an electrical engineering major, turned to fellow student Jamelle Smith.

"Jamelle, you've got just a little cottage cheese around your mouth."

"Oh, thanks," said Jamelle, wiping his mouth with a napkin. "Sorry." The biology major sighed and admitted, "I can't afford to buy my books till next payday." Nineteen-year-old Jamelle, a black student with long, braided hair, shook his head in embarrassment. He worked part-time as a cashier at Boxed-Up Biggies, a leading big-box store on Wabash Avenue in Springfield.

"Geez, I feel privileged," admitted Lisa Westman, a social services major. Her wealthy parents, who expected her to become a business major and career woman, were dismayed by her choice.

"My parents bought my books." She looked down as she said this. Lisa, a liberal, down-to-earth Thronez, yearned to be accepted among the lower middle-class college crowd. "But my car just broke down," Lisa added, attempting to redeem herself, "and there's no way I'm asking Mom and Dad to fix it." Lisa always tried to distance herself from her white-collar parents, maintaining a blue-collar outlook. She volunteered at the Red Cross and the Springfield Homeless Shelter, avoiding the capitalistic path her parents had tried to set for her.

Oliver Rhodes chimed in, "Listen, guys. Let's face it. The goal of the capitalist cigar snuffers is to determine and then orchestrate the lowest possible standard of living that can be tolerated by the masses before demonstrations and riots take place. When the population reaches that level—that trough—the industrial bastards hold to it tightly to maximize their share of the financial pie and minimize the workers' share. For example, my job at Happy Hamburger pays about the lowest I will go before I start tossing bricks through windows. You see, those

Conservapricks are squeezing tightly with their little butthole muscles so as not to give anything more than they have to."

They intend to relinquish nothing extra to us proletariats. Their dispassionate sphincters are just quivering with dread at the thought of having to share the wealth." Everyone at the table laughed as Oliver stretched his facial features to the max to illustrate stinginess and prissiness. "They go masquerading around in their little three-piece clown suits—their 'capitalist costumes,' as the late Wilbert Noah Stokes put it—trying to convince everyone that they are fair and honest white men whose intentions are directed toward the preservation and even the advancement of the common man. But, of course, you know that's just toilet talk. They wave the American Dream and Diversity flags in our faces, knowing full well it is only one in a thousand who will escape the peon pit we all swim in. It's an old, conservative, rich white man's government, and we all know it." They will keep us all at the brim of poverty, tossing a few morsels of fish food to those who manage to temporarily rise to the surface, but otherwise live in the permanence of financial incarceration."

Lisa Westman sized-up Oliver with adoring eyes. She just loved the way he could pick apart a situation and expose its sinister inner workings so that lower mankind might emerge from the suffocating oppression contrived upon it by the global elite. In summary, Lisa had a queen-size crush on the intense-talking neo-hippie and his efforts to deconstruct the mechanisms of human control by the corporate hogs.

"Your analysis is quite impressive," Lisa would say at the conclusion of one of Oliver's harangues.

"But none of us are poor, Oliver," responded Jamelle. "We've all got shoes and socks, cellphones and CD players. Don't we?" Jamelle looked around the table.

"But dude, you could have more!" squawked Randy. "I, for one, am always broke. Every time I'm ready to get ahead, something happens to put me right back into the poorhouse."

"We're all struggling, Randy, Oliver," explained Martha, "but don't you think that the notion of 'riots' is a bit too strong? I mean, my parents started out poor but slowly built up wealth and aren't doing badly at this point. I don't know how much money they have, but they could certainly afford to send me to college. And my job at the mall is no better than your job at Happy Hamburger, but—"

"And I appreciate that," said Oliver, "but the industrialists and the information crunchers love when you talk that way, Martha. They want you to be barely content. It's fine if all you want to do in life is eat your spicy Vegan Platter, doodle around on your smartphone, and be swallowed up by a few silly sitcoms. But I just want a little more out of life."

"I'm slightly offended," retorted Martha.

"Sorry," said Oliver. "Didn't mean anything personal by it."

"I just don't approve of 'tossing bricks through windows,'" noted Martha.

"I didn't mean that literally, Martha," said Oliver.

"You mentioned Wilbert something," said Jamelle. "Who's that?"

"Wilbert Noah Stokes," replied Oliver. "He was just an old hippie guy from the 1970s. He was quoted in the book *The Post-*

Vietnam Hippie Guide to the Streets: How to Survive the Punk-Rock Era."

"Hmmm," noted Jamelle, "but I like punk and new wave music."

"I do too," said Oliver. "I just like psychedelic music a little more. The book is just kind of a humorous examination of later hippiedom." Oliver smiled. "You see, Wilbert lived in a day before cellphones and the internet. He knew how to communicate directly with people." Oliver took a gulp of his coffee. "You know, I went to get an oil change for my mom's car yesterday, and nobody spoke a word to anyone else in the waiting room of the car dealership. Everyone just sat there like dumbasses, playing with their smartphones. Not too long ago, the place would have been buzzing with conversation. But now it's just all silos, everyone on their own planet. This world is doomed."

Oliver drank the last of his coffee and grimaced. "Yuck! Cold coffee."

"And yes, punk rock is way better than what we have now. This is the worst era in rock history, even worse than the early 60s before the Beatles, Rolling Stones, The Byrds, Dylan, and the Kinks changed everything. I haven't heard a great album since Beck's *Sea Change* in what, 2002? I'm afraid rock is basically dead."

"Yeah," agreed Jamelle, "there's nothing like The Beatles or Stones nowadays. It's all pretty lame—just a bunch of glittery solo artists singing top 40 muck."

After Randy, Martha, and Jamelle went their separate ways, Oliver asked Lisa out in front of the boring backlit sign Ray's had put up in place of the wonderful old neon sign. Lisa was thrilled, and they planned to meet that Friday at Oliver's house to watch a movie.

"You can meet my mom and my cat, Phoenix," said Oliver. "He's a far-out creature. You'll like him."

"I look forward to it," smiled Lisa. "Oh, and I am not a slave to my cellphone."

"You are not, indeed," replied a pleased Oliver.

The sinking sun cast long shadows on the concrete pavement, the colorful signage, and the parked cars in the heart of old Springfield. Meanwhile, a mild buzz filled both lovestruck students' heads as they departed.

Half of the group had dispersed for good. Randy dropped out of school, became a heavy drinker, and hung around with his new, jobless, alcoholic friends.

Martha thought Oliver too weird and did not come around anymore. Jamelle, however, remained Oliver's faithful friend.

TUG OF WAR

"Hello there, are you interested in some company?" asked a bleach-blonde woman smoking a Marlboro cigarette, looking up into the cab of the semi-truck.

"What's the price?" inquired Douglas "Tug" McRae, a burly and hairy truck driver with crooked teeth and a constant scowl.

"What do you want? For straight sex, $150. For—"

"Put out that smoke 'n' jump on in."

As Tug rolled up the driver's side window of his rig, Tanya briskly walked around to the passenger door. Tug unlocked it, and Tanya opened it.

"What's your name?" she asked with a forced kindness.

"I'm Tug," said the brawny trucker with a scruffy beard, short wavy hair, and a mildly bulbous nose.

"I'm Tanya," she said proudly, slamming the door of the oversized cab shut. "So, what can I do for you, Tug?"

"I'll suck that fat cock of yours for $80."

"How do you know it's fat?"

"You're a big man."

"Yer just the kind of sassy bitch I've been lookin' for. "Come on back," he motioned, lifting his hulking frame from the plush but sunken seat and lumbering to the back of the cab.

Tug's cellphone rang. "Hello?" he barked.

"Tuggy," his mother, Alice, announced, "I've got some new medicine for your hemorrhoids."

"Mom, I'm working. I don't have time to talk about it!" He hung up the phone, while Tanya, who overheard Alice McRae's shrill voice, tried to muffle her giggling.

A dim night light guided Tanya to the bed in the back, where she began taking off her blouse. "I do charge up front," she stated firmly.

Tug handed her a wad of $20 bills, telling the night prowler, "I'll take straight sex. Here's $160. Keep the change." Then he switched off the night light, pulled a ski mask over his large face, and slipped his arms into a size XXL flannel shirt.

"I prefer you leave the light on," said the suspicious harlot.

Ignoring the blonde hooker, Tug pressed the PLAY button on his portable tape machine. A strong voice boomed out the words of a half-crazed man. "THIS IS BULK BOGUS, AND FOLKS, I'M HERE TO TELL YOU THAT COWBOY BENNY IS NOTHIN' BUT A LOWDOWN COWARD! HE'S BEEN DUCKIN' ME AT EVERY TURN!"

"What are you doing?" demanded Tanya. "Alright, no funny business, buster! Let me out!" Tug found her and grabbed her bony arms. Abruptly, she cried again, "What are you do--?"

"—"THAT FAT OX THINKS HE'S GONNA BULLY ME? WELL, I'VE GOT SOMETHING I'M GONNA SINK INTO HIS BIG UGLY FACE! MY FIST! AND THAT DUMB ASS WILL DO NOTHING ABOUT IT, 'CAUSE I'M GONNA RIP HIS—"

"I'm getting out of he—" screamed Tanya.

Tug took hold of her throat with both hands. She gagged and squirmed. She tried to scratch Tug's face and arms but could not penetrate his protection. She flailed madly for a moment, face blue, eyes watering. She found great strength, but fighting off a huge man like Tug was beyond her. Gradually, her flailing died down. Finally, she began to turn limp. Tug eased up on his grip, grabbed a sock and began stuffing it in her mouth. Tanya groaned and struggled to cough. By now, she realized the recording was the voice of a well-known professional wrestling star. "I'LL FIGHT THAT BIG STUPID CLOD ANYTIME! BRING IT ON, DUMBO!!!" Tanya again coughed and gagged. She thought about her two children, and a tear dripped from her right eye.

Tug quickly unzipped his trousers and placed a plastic bread bag around his swollen penis, while holding Tanya down by the throat with one brawny hand. He secured the bag with a rubber band, mimicking the strangulation of his victim by pulling the band tight and wrapping another loop around the organ. He manipulated the band with a single hand the way an acrobat might do it.

Now Tug took a bungee cord from a hook on the cab wall and wrapped it around Tanya's thin neck—not too tightly—but just enough to let her gag again. She opened her eyes widely like a startled cat. She moaned with primeval misery, as Tug pulled the bungee cord tighter, making a new rotation around her taut neck. The itching in Tug's groin grew almost intolerable. Tanya passed out again, and he toyed with her, easing up on the cord, then applying another revolution around her neck. He did so repeatedly until she did not come back. Realizing she was gone, and before he would ever have time to mount her, he commenced to ejaculate into the plastic bread bag. By now he knew, with Tanya being his third victim that he could not hold off on completing himself. He wanted so much to penetrate the new corpse, yet he knew from experience that he would ejaculate before he desired.

He unwound the bungee cord and threw it aside, then placed both thumbs at the center of Tanya's neck and squeezed with the force of a fully-tightened vice, trying to revisit his crime, letting out a blood-chilling grunt as he ejaculated into the bread bag for a second time. He collapsed beside Tanya on the bed. He breathed heavily for a moment, as the ranting voice of Bulk Bogus continued to pollute the air. "I'M THE GREATEST WRESTLER OF ALL TIME! I'M INVINCIBLE!"

After another moment, Tug picked himself up, removed the shirt and mask, and finally pressed the stop button on the tape machine.

Here, the big man grabbed a folded green chemical suit from a nightstand, which was bolted to the wall of the cab. He unfolded the suit and put his large self into it.

"Sugar," said Tug to Tanya's corpse, "you were jus' too sweet." He let out a demented laugh, more of a howl really, then put on a red baseball cap with the white letters "MAWA" across the front.

Before he even bothered to dispose of the corpse, Tug dialed a number on his smartphone.

"Hello," said a casual-sounding voice on the other end.

"Hey doll, what's up?"

"Hello sweetie, how can I help you?"

"You want to hook up?" asked Tug.

"What's yer name, sweetie."

"Tug. How 'bout a date."

"How didja get my number, Tug?"

"Um, I saw your internet ad," Tug lied.

"I don't have an internet ad."

"Well, what does it matter? I'm a paying customer."

"Jus' want to make sure you're not a cop."

"I'm not a cop. I'm drivin' a big rig, for Gore's sake!"

"Why didn't you say so, sweetie."

"I love when you talk to me that way, doll."

"I'm at the Prime Motel in Collinsville right now. Can you meet me here?"

"How 'bout an hour from now? I gotta dispose of somethin', then I'll be headin' your way." The large man grinned like some demented child. "Cicely, right?"

"That's me, sweetie. I'll see you in the west parking lot. You can park your truck there. I've got on jeans and a red top. See you there, sweetie."

"OK, bye."

Tug was too embarrassed to buy condoms at the corner drugstore, or even at the local Floor-Mart. "You can't even buy 'em from machines anymore," he complained in a low voice. Tug came up with the empty bread bag idea after he suffocated a prostitute by using a round-loaf bag over her head. When he feels the need to ejaculate, which is every time he finds a fresh corpse at the tips of his thick fingers, he simply whips out a bread bag from his pocket with a rubber band inside. He digs out the rubber band, places the bread bag over his enlarged member, and wraps it single-handedly with the precision of an Eagle Scout. Tug laughed again as he thought about it.

Meanwhile, shimmering stars, suddenly obscured by a fast-moving cloud, lamented the perilous moment. The soft light of a half-moon revealed the red button with white letters on Tug's discarded flannel shirt. It read, "Vote for Ghant Wackersham! Conservaprick Candidate."

THE TWO MELS

"Oh, Buttercup," said Melvin Goodall to his stunningly beautiful wife, Melanie, "what shall we do on this blessed summer day?"

"Well, darling," said Melanie, "I thought we would stop by the Wackersham Campaign Headquarters and pick up some signs."

"Why, Buttercup, that sounds marvelous! And let us do some window-shopping in the Blandon Mall. I need to find a gift for Uncle Owen."

"Sure, dear," agreed Melanie, "and maybe afterwards we can bring some doughnuts home and listen to Lawrence Welk records."

"That sounds delightful, Buttercup. Just splendid!"

Their Double-Income-No-Kids status made the meticulous financial advisor and his perpetually optimistic real estate agent wife a wealthy couple. Their country estate with a backyard pond and a two-hole golf course sat at the outer east edge of pleasant Blandon, Illinois.

"We both have 9-to-5 careers," Melvin would boast, "and neither of us has to drive through the black neighborhood to get to our jobs." The second part of the sentence, of course, was spoken in a whisper.

"That's right," noted Melanie from behind an exhaustive make-up job. "We live on the *East* Side." She glowed like a sparkler on an overcast night when she said this.

Melvin had dark red hair and a few freckles on his cheeks. Melanie was a brunette with shiny eyes, a generous figure, and a determined smile. They both wore smartphone headsets with microphones, seeming like extensions of their bodies. Onlookers might have guessed that the quintessential all-American couple ate dinner, went shopping, and even had sex with their headsets still on.

Both Melvin and Melanie exhibited remarkable hubris, much like their favorite Conservaprick presidential candidate, Ghant Wackersham.

They firmly believed that loyal, conservative Americans, next to Thronez, represent the paragon of humanity and could say or do as they pleased, no matter the pain inflicted upon any challenger, who proved an adversary to "clean" living and virtuous behavior. And they adhered to the conservative principles of the Spongez Church, holding a special place at the pinnacle of white Gorebingerz society.

In public, the Spongez couple was known as "The Two Mels." In private, they were referred to as the "Golden Pair." They did everything together, including square dancing, campaigning for their favorite Conservaprick candidate, and playing croquet. They even soaked their feet together, admiring how their sparkling white toes made for a grand set.

And they both had visions of their part in The Rapture, the time when all good Spongez would follow the Thronez, from the land of Quasar, straight up to heaven at the commencement of the End of Times. They both thought the hour had arrived when America commenced to a War of Lies revolving around the fabricated premise that Irad had WMDs (Wagons of Miniscule Duds, it turned out). In fact, it amused Melvin to think that the war in Irad could possibly hasten The Rapture, despite the exaggerations and outright lies that propelled American forces into that dismal experience, ultimately claiming the lives of about 800,000 people. So, The Two Mels cheer-leaded the conflict in Irad that it might serve as a prequel, or springboard, to their rising to heaven, but the Rapture never quite materialized. Still, they held great hope that future conflicts would achieve their objective. And the prospect that Ghant Wackersham, the 2028 Conservaprick candidate, could orchestrate a renewed effort to trigger The Rapture thrilled all loyal Spongez followers.

May their journeys skyward engender a most pleasurable ride.

Milking the Prole

"Hello, my name is Elma Ray and I need to file a claim for unemployment," said the laid-off African-American worker on the calling end of the telephone.

She had just survived four weeks of training her Indian replacement and now was officially unemployed. Meanwhile, she had been sending out resumes to various companies and even applied to a motel maid position to tide her over until she could find a comparable computer programming position like the one she had at Monroe-Belkamp Inc., in their esteemed IT Department.

"Is that right?" said Elma. "Well then, I'll sign-up at the web site. You say w w w dot--Ok, got it! Thank you ma'am. Bye." Elma hung up the phone with her right hand, then she lifted it with her left hand and quickly hung it up again. She could not allow her right to go unanswered.

Elma Ray did not exhibit the bitterness that her co-worker, Phillip Troutman did before he filled out his last timesheet. "Those filthy corporate scoundrels," Phillip barked, "This is part of their plan to lower wages for the entire computer industry. The result is a surplus of unemployed American programmers who will have to accept less money to find another position. They used me up, then spit me out for an Indian. Now, mind you, I have nothing against the Indian people. They're mostly all nice people. No, I blame it on the disgraceful American corporation! They squeezed me like a sponge for 28 years, then tossed me in the shitcan like a snotty tissue."

Now Elma and her son Tyrel would have to watch their spending. Life was about to undergo significant changes.

Saturday movie outings and generous church donations would be put on hold. Trips to the We Are Toys store and Tyrel's drum lessons would also be suspended. Despite these challenges, Elma remained optimistic, believing that good things happen to those who work hard and live with integrity.

Phillip Troutman expressed his strong concerns to his brother-in-law, worried about the impact on wages and job security. He felt that the situation was unfair and that promises had been broken. He was concerned that the involvement of foreign workers would negatively impact local employment.

"Fuck those slimy corporate bastards! I hope industrialized America sodomizes itself so hard, its dick comes out of its own mouth!!! Goddamnit, I wasn't ready to retire yet. I had three more fucking years!"

Meanwhile, Elma reached out to her friend Maria, who had recently made a career transition from a bank teller to a hostess at the upscale Horatio's Restaurante, located in the affluent East side of Blandon-Average, a twin city in Illinois. This area was fondly referred to as "The Cream Puff District" or "Bubbledumb" by Oliver Rhodes, the young man from Springfield. They talked about weather and family and finally the conversation drifted toward Presidential bad-boy hopeful, Ghant Wackersham.

"If that guy gets in, we're all sunk," Maria stated.

"Yeah, you know," said Elma, "I want our president to be *better* than me…to have more accomplishments and just be a better person. But this guy…."

"Oh, he's repulsive and vulgar," injected Maria.

"And he lies so effortlessly," added Elma.

"Could you imagine living under his rule?" asked Maria. "He's so fascist. He's worse than President Schmidt ever was. And Schmidt was *baaaaad*."

Elma peered out the living room window and sighed at all of the Conservaprick signs in the neighborhood. They all just said "Ghant!" That one word with exclamation was enough to shake any decent one's world, to cloud any sane person's outlook on future America.

Rubber Cheese

"Hi mom, I'm starving," said Oliver Rhodes as he walked through the front door of the small bungalow on Canopy Street in the city of Springfield, Illinois. Oliver, with his long brown hair parted down the middle and a thin mustache, had a lean and lanky physique. His living room was a testament to his eclectic style, with worn furniture that seemed to be barely holding on. The couch, propped up by a stack of three books, looked like it was on the verge of collapse. The recliner, adorned with a vibrant tapestry, was a constant source of fascination for Oliver, especially after a few hits of marijuana. The old tube TV, a relic of a bygone era, seemed like a dinosaur in the modern age. The coffee table in front of the couch was cluttered with knick-knacks and the day's mail, which consisted of a few bills and a magazine, adding to the overall sense of chaos and disarray. A single cigarette burn shouted out its prominence on the side of the table facing the kitchen, probably a leftover from Mandy's days of smoking. A half shelf strewn with paperback novels stood next to the fat tube of the television. A tattered throw rug, adorned with a psychedelic pattern of multicolored circles, added a touch of surrealism to the room. Oliver loved to gaze at it when he was, ahem, "enhanced" by his favorite herb. The rug supported the table, which was a feat in itself. Meanwhile, a lazy cobweb hung in the northwest corner, looking like a forgotten party decoration. And, as a nod to the household's feline overlord, Phoenix, a cloth mouse toy with oversized ears lay abandoned on the rug, as if it had been suddenly fleeing from the chaos that was Oliver's living room. The place could be dismal in appearance, yet Oliver often longed for this home when he was away. He tried to stave off the embarrassment he felt when his girlfriend, Lisa Westman, visited the dreary, Section 8 castle.

"Hi son," said Oliver's mother, Mandy Jo Hicks, "there's some stew in the fridge you can heat up." Mandy wore wavy brown hair and could be described as a tad dumpy in physical character, though she was quite friendly and honest, a blithesome soul.

"Whatcha readin'?" asked Oliver.

"Oh, just some stuff from the Allcon Church."

"Mom, I told you, that material can be hazardous to your mind. It's the corniest of all the religions. Besides, I thought you were supposed to be a Southern Badpest."

"I am, Oliver. Can't I just look?"

"Mom, some nineteenth-century imposter made up that religion."

"Oh, Oliver, I wish you wouldn't."

"Well, at least the Gorebingerz faith is a couple thousand years old. At least they've got that going for them. But the Allcon branch of it is a modern fraud."

"Does this mean I'm in for another Oliver spiel?"

"Mom, all modern violence is rooted in the Babble. It's the most violent and treacherous book ever written. The guys who got together and wrote it gave purpose to every violent act ever committed."

"What do you mean, 'The guys who got together and wrote it?'"

"A bunch of wise, old zealots gathered in a room and wrote the thing. They're highly educated individuals, mother. Mensa material, and a bit crazy. Many brilliant minds are a bit eccentric, lacking in practical sense, but exceptionally book smart. Didn't you know that? However, they often struggle with spiritual depth."

"Oliver, they're not crazy!" his mother protested.

"Ah, but many masterminds are indeed unhinged, mother. Think of your serial killers and terrorists - they're often genius-level intellects. Their minds are wired differently, overflowing with ideas and complexities."

"What's Mensa?"

"A group of very smart people. They write manifestos and Babbles and such."

"Son, God wrote the Babble." Mandy paused for a moment, then reluctantly corrected herself.

"Well, maybe He didn't *write* it, but it's *His* words."

"No offense, mom. I'm not saying 'Don't believe in a God.' I'm just saying that much of the Babble is nonsense. "Passed down from old folk tales," Oliver said with a sly grin, "and embellished, embellished, and embellished." His mother's expression turned stern, and she raised a hand to silence him.

"That's enough, Oliver! I don't want to hear any more!" she exclaimed, her patience worn thin.

Oliver chuckled and shrugged, "OK, mom. Go on with what you were doing before I came home." He tossed his college books onto the living room table, the sound echoing through the room, and sauntered into the kitchen, leaving his mother to her exasperation.

"Do we have any more of that rubber cheese?" he asked.

"Rubber cheese?" Mandy Jo's voice trembled, as she was so upset.

"You know, the cheap stuff we got from Floor-Mart." Oliver put some stew on the stove, made himself a ham-and-cheese sandwich, and plopped on the living room couch next to his mother.

"Don't!" cried Mandy. "You're messin' up my papers!"

Oliver's gaze fell upon a campaign pamphlet for Ghant Wackersham, the Conservaprick candidate. His expression turned scornful. "Can you believe this guy is vying for the highest office in the land? He's a complete charlatan! His supporters think he's The Peerless Profit - spelled P-R-O-F-I-T, no less."

His mother chided him, "Oliver, your father would disapprove of such language."

Oliver's response was laced with sarcasm. "Ah, yes, my father - the one who abandoned us when I was nine. I wouldn't put much stock in his opinions, anyway. His opinion sucks!"

"Oliver, many folks believe Ghant Wackersham has been heavenly sent."

"And they're all full of fucking hot shit!"

"Oliver, please don't put your feet on the table."

Oliver retired to his room and called his girlfriend, Lisa Westman, to vent about his mom reading Allcon literature.

"Hello, Lisa?"

"Hi Oliver, how was your day?"

"Good…until I caught mom reading Allcon writings."

"Uh-oh, hon', you didn't get yourself into trouble again, I hope."

"Well, no, but mom didn't like what I had to say." Oliver stroked the third member of the Hicks household, Phoenix, the cat.

Oliver's beloved cat, Phoenix, got his name from his remarkable rescue story. Found dying under a bridge, Phoenix was a flea-infested, skin-infected bundle of bones. But with Oliver's devoted care and veterinary treatment, he made a miraculous recovery, rising like a phoenix from the ashes. The once-sickly cat transformed into a vibrant, quirky companion, with a personality as unpredictable as a screwball. Phoenix defied feline norms by loving car rides, sitting up like a dog on Oliver's lap, and gazing out the window at the passing world. At home, he ruled, insisting on open doors and cabinets, and refusing to compromise on his Egyptian Sands cat litter. Oliver laughed, "But Gore, it's killing me!" - a testament to the cat's endearing yet demanding nature.

"Those Allcons are one of the all-time religious-organization phonies. Mass retardation, I tell you. Some self-proclaimed Prophet supposedly uncovered --."

"But Oliver, you've got to take it easy with your mom. You know she gets upset when you make fun of religion."

"I know, I know, I can't resist a good tale. So, the self-proclaimed Allcon Prophet allegedly unearthed some ancient chamber pots in a South Chicago landfill. And, lo and behold, the pots bore the sacred Tablet of Allcons. The Allcons proclaimed themselves the new Angels, but their holier-than-thou attitude and penchant for petty theft got them booted from several states. Eventually, they settled in the quirky State of Plastic Utopia, where they somehow managed to gain a following and achieve success." Oliver's tone was laced with a mix of amusement and skepticism.

Lisa laughed. "Now hon', don't get too worked up. And keep that stuff to yourself, please."

"I guess…."

"Did you see the launching of the spaceship, Aster, today?" asked Lisa.

"Fuck this going-to-the-moon shit," snapped Oliver. "What do I care if they make it to the moon, Jupiter, Pluto or the next galaxy? "If they ever discover another planet to exploit, it'll be the deceitful, manipulative politicians who'll get to escape Earth, not ordinary people like us. We'll be left behind, struggling to survive. It's infuriating to think that our hard-earned tax dollars might fund a luxurious getaway for the likes of Wackersham, while we're stuck here, fighting to make ends meet. I work tirelessly at Happy Hamburger, and the thought of subsidizing an elitist's intergalactic adventure with my taxes is utterly appalling."

"Geez, Oliver, I'm sorry you called. I didn't know you'd be so crabby."

"Sorry. I really am. You don't deserve such talk, Lisa. Hey, I got a joke for you. How many capitalists does it take to change a light bulb?"

"I don't know, Oliver. How many?"

"The answer is none. It takes zero capitalists to change a light bulb."

"I don't get it."

"They sold the new light bulb to the highest bidder. So it took no one to change it."

Lisa giggled.

"Here's one I thought up today," said Oliver. "The power elite maintains control over the population through four primary mechanisms: spicy food, technological gadgetry, charming television commercials, and the Great American Sitcom. Once these influences are deeply ingrained, the average citizen becomes apathetic towards government actions, including the invasion of innocent nations, the poisoning of water sources by chemical corporations, and the destruction of land by oil conglomerates. The populace is effectively sedated, distracted from the truth, and reduced to a state of compliance."

The American citizen just doesn't care if he or she has got their tech toy, spicey double-onion, triple-grease sandwich, and a string of commercials trying to out-cute each other, all anchored by a bad Shit-Com show. It keeps the masses contented."

"Oliver, you're weird," said Lisa, "but that's why I like you so much!"

"You sure about that? You would never catch me at a prom, wearing one of those retarded graduation caps, letting someone style my hair, enjoying a television commercial, making somebody sit through my wedding, having brunch, celebrating Valentine's Day, or attending a political rally. You still like me?"

"Yes. I don't care about any of those things either."

Posting Eyeballs

When Tug reached a point on the highway where thick forests flanked the road, he stopped the big blue truck and dragged Tanya's corpse to the edge of the woods. He laid her aside some trees where he was just out of sight of any vehicles passing by, and began his second ritual. He removed a pair of double-edged sticks from the quiver strapped around his shoulder and planted one end of each firmly in the ground. There they stood in the dark like a pair of goal posts sans crossbar. He then removed a gardening trowel from his tool belt and proceeded to dig out the eyeballs from Tanya's head. First, he shoveled out the right eye and planted it on top of the stick on the left. Then he shoveled out the left eye and planted it on top of the stick on the right. The noise sounded like someone breaking apart a couple of cabbages. This was no surgical procedure, but a very sloppy affair.

Next, Tug removed her jeans and panties. He took a douche from his tool belt and ensconced the nozzle firmly in the poor girl's vagina. He gave the bag a quick squeeze and filled the girl with the prepackaged solution. He then removed the sock from her mouth, and prepared to extract a trophy. He removed Tanya's shoes and socks and laid them out next to her body. He took a pair of long-nosed pliers from his tool belt, examined the big toe of each foot, and deciding on the right foot, he tightly gripped the nail of the big toe and ripped it out of its snug place. He then wiped the toe nail on his chemical suit, inserted the thing in the sock he had pulled from her mouth, and stuffed it in his pants pocket. He looked down on Tanya's leather fringed purse, still around her shoulder, and exclaimed, "I fucking hate hippies!"

Now he removed the green chemical gown and left it on the ground. Finally, he turned andcasually walked back to his truck.

He climbed back inside the huge cab, pulled out a bag of peanuts, and began munching them between his big molars. Tug couldn't resist the urge to polish his shirt's button with a napkin, essentially mocking the Conservaprick's reverence for their leader. To them, Wackersham was a paragon of excellence, a divine gift to the world of politics. Oliver had sarcastically dubbed him "The Peerless Profit." Wackersham's support base consisted of two primary groups: the obscenely wealthy, who believed he would lead them to even greater riches, and the impoverished masses, who naively thought that merely touching him - whether through their TV screens or at his rallies - would bring them good fortune and advancement in their mundane, low-paying jobs. These mill-rats and lowly store clerks were the blue-collar voters the Librhoid Party had lost to the Conservapricks. Both groups, rich and poor, thought they deserved something special for being white. Of course, there were the tag-alongs—people who pretended to have lots of money and class, though they had neither.

Tug's face wore a confident smile, convinced that Ghant's success would trickle down to him. Like his friends back in Wheeling, Illinois, he had invested heavily in stocks, swept up in the frenzy surrounding Wackersham's potential election. "Wackersham's gonna make us all rich!" he boasted to his pals.

But they were oblivious to the fact that Wackersham and his sixteen corporations would reap massive profits, while their own investments eventually stagnated after enduring a volatile market.

Tug surveyed his tricked-out truck cab, already equipped with a microwave, stereo, bed, and TV. He envisioned even more upgrades, like a CD and DVD player, as his profits soared. His latest 401K statement had him dreaming of a Wackersham victory, and the windfall that would surely follow. Little did he know, the fog of questionable finances would soon engulf Wackersham's empire, leaving him and his friends in a sea of financial uncertainty.

At that very moment his mother called. "Tuggy, I have some exciting news for you, son."

"Oh yeah, what's that?" the shameless murderer asked.

"Ghant is coming to Central Illinois!"

"Great! When's that?"

"Next month, dear. August 6th. He'll be speaking at the University in the town of Average."

"OK, mom. Thanks for the awesome news! Gotta go now. Gotta meet someone. Bye."

As Tug got back on the road, he lost himself in the rhythm of the white dashed lines on the highway. He began to reflect on his actions and his peculiar hobby, feeling a growing determination to change his murderous ways. "Dammit, I'm going to be different!" he insisted to himself. "I can't just be another stereotypical truck-driving serial killer. I need to come up with new methods, new ideas."

Even in the dark, Tug noticed the rows of "Ghant!" signs along the expressway. "We'll roll 'em over," he chuckled, thinking about the ill-fated Librhoid Party.

In that moment, everything felt right in the cab of his semi-truck.

Tug smiled like a happy child, then went back to his normal scowl. The night hung low and damp like a tiny toad on a water lily.

DINK NOOKY

After dining on their clam cakes Melvin and Melanie settled down on the family-room sofa with a glass of $200-a-bottle red wine. They watched a DVD of a sermon by Dr. Torrance Van Irwin, a renowned and animated Spongez preacher, and settled in for the evening.

Melvin lay on the $3,000 sofa, his feet draped across Melanie's lap. The painted seductress tickled his feet while Dr. Van Irwin passionately delivered his Babblical teachings. As Melvin giggled, he was transported back to his youth, recalling how his mother would gently brush his toes with her fingernails. Those memories of childhood felt enchanting. Melanie's gentle caresses on the balls of his feet brought Melvin a sense of relaxation and nostalgia, causing him to giggle and then experience a mild arousal.

He tried to squeeze one of Melanie's nipples between his toes but could not maneuver the little pink appendages into the proper angle. Melanie now giggled briefly.

Once the video terminated Melvin felt antsy. He cuddled up to his heavily made-up spouse and fidgeted a bit with a button on her white blouse.

"Mel, honey," Melanie said, "are you in one of your romantic moods?"

The embarrassed Spongez felt his puny muscle quiver. "Well, Buttercup," said he, "if you don't mind."

"Darling, I don't ever mind. Come here my little birdie." Before long, Melvin kissed and fondled Melanie's ripe breasts, while stripping off his trousers. The foreplay continued as the wine played its magic in the candle-lit family room. Silk blankets barely rustled as the two kissed like high school sweethearts.

Melvin breathed heavily and whispered, "Oh, baby, put on those glittery Floor-Mart slippers…and those junk-metal Woolworth's earrings…and make fabulous love to me."

"But dear," Melanie weakly protested, "don't you like these $200 Jayman Martus slippers? I just bought them." Melvin only breathed passionately. Melanie added, "And this gown, dear, how do you like it? I paid $465 on sale!"

"No, baby, put on that flimsy Sex Kitten gown you bought at Kinky Sam's."

"Oh, Melvin!"

"Oooohhh, to make love to you in the back seat of a Ford Pinto!"

"But dear, this plush bed linen only cost $829. But—yum, yum—got it on sale for $795."

"Oh, let's just pretend we're in the back seat of a Pinto, Melanie, my love! Can't you just imagine?"

Sloppy kissing suction sounds decorated the dim room. "Anything you say dear," moaned Melanie.

"Oh, baby, do it to meeeeeeee!" cried Melvin. "Oh, oh, Blast off!"

The two lovers embraced as Melvin experienced a thunderous orgasmic storm. Then, panting like a little pup, he plopped down on the silk bedding and continued to breath heavily. His tiny member shriveled into an acorn.

"You were wonderful, dear," sighed Melanie, as she felt an urgent need to masturbate herself into completion. Of course, she refrained.

"Thanks, darling," said Melvin. "Just don't ever tell anyone about the sensitivities of my sexual yearnings. It might ruin our image." Melvin struggled to catch his breath and was embarrassed that such little exertion made him respire so deeply. "Just think what that could do to our standing in the Conservaprick Party. Oh, and if the Librhoids ever got a hold of it, not even the Rapture could save us!"

Melanie swore she would not tell. Yet, soon she was relaying to her friend, Carla, on the telephone, how "Melvin has a sort of…little pee-pee, if you know what I mean. But, it's what he does with it that's so special." The two phone mates would then giggle delightedly.

The pair of love-struck Spongez were soon in bed, dozing to the soft sounds of the wind chimes on their front porch. Everything was dandy in the Goodall household. Melvin and Melanie's sweet souls slept soundly beneath the Ghant Wackersham picture on the big posterboard hanging next to the $6,000 canopy-with-curtains bed, an awkward sight among the $1000 lamps and matching cherry nightstands, part of a $27,000 bedroom set. Wackersham's dyed black hair looked like it was plastered onto his head. His narrow eyes and arrogant smile went well with that conservative outfit, that famous Capitalist Costume: the three-piece suit.

Drudgery for Paradiddles

Just Elma's luck it was that the economy would tank as she searched for work. Reluctantly, she accepted the motel-maid position at Sparky's Paradise Inn, one of the few remaining mom-and-pop motels left in the Prairie State, which no longer had much prairie to brag about, though the name still clung to ancient threads. Too many long, tedious hours had she slumped over her college books for this motel labor to feel enriching in any way. Too many sleep-deprived nights had she studied beneath the lamp in her tiny, closet-like room at Cornland University in Blandon-Average to derive any satisfaction from this temporary position. But here she was, knowing she had to find some sense of worth, some glimmer of value from such laborious work. After all, she had a child to feed, clothe, and nurture into a level-headed adult.

So, Elma mopped with her right hand, then switched to her left. She wiped out the bathroom sink with one hand and then again with the other. She alternated hands while rolling the vacuum cleaner up and down the rooms, the halls, and the entryway. She flicked on a light switch with one hand and turned it off with the other. Now and then, she would call young Tyrel, hoping to catch him during a break from his drum practice.

The semi-seedy premises of Sparky's Paradise Inn she would not allow to irk her. The occasional shady character she would not fear, as she knew everybody needed some kind of home, even the downtrodden, long-term clientele of Sparky's. Elma's spirit remained untainted by the dingy "palace" she worked in or her seemingly aimless existence. She had faced worse before. Besides, the owners were friendly, and she desperately needed the pay.

Then, one evening, she came home to find a foreclosure notice in her mailbox. Where would they go? Where would Tyrel practice his paradiddles? Her situation seemed bleak, yet she reassured herself that everything would be alright. She just knew it.

Only yesterday, she had witnessed the dreary prospects of others when she helped break up a fight at Floor-Mart. Two hillbilly women were battling over the last package of frozen corndogs, clawing at each other desperately, screeching obscenities, and yanking out clumps of hair like crumpled cutting paper from an Easter basket.

There they were with ripped shirts, half-exposed breasts and facial lacerations, panting heavily as their fellow shoppers and then a security guard held them apart. At this moment Elma thought of her condition as quite elevated from that of these sorry, bleeding combatants.

The Tug Bug

"Oliver, I met someone online," blurted an excited Mandy Jo.

"Oh yeah?

What's his name?"

"Tug."

"Sounds like a boat," remarked Oliver with sarcasm. "Oh Oliver, you're so silly."

"What does he do for a living?"

"He's a truck driver. He drives a semi."

"Hmmm. Where does he live?"

"Up by Chicago."

"Mom, we're in Springfield. How are you gonna get up there?"

"He's coming here."

"To this house?"

"No, no. I'm gonna meet him at McDonald's. I won't invite him here until I'm sure I can trust him."

"Well," said Oliver, "I guess I'm happy for you. Just be careful. There are some real nuts hanging around the internet these days." He paused to open a package of Harold Buttquick ham.

"What do you guys have in common?"

"You're not gonna like it, dear."

"Don't tell me. Ghant Wackersham?"

"How did you guess, you stinker."

"Well," mused Oliver, "right off the bat I don't trust him."

"Now Oliver, don't start."

"Mom, today's Conservaprick Party is made up of thugs. And Ghant Wackersham is the wanna-be head thug. He's a dictator in-the-making. I mean, didn't you get enough of that from President Schmidt?"

"That's your opinion, son. Don't take it out on Tug."

"Tug the Thug," said Oliver.

"Alright, I've had enough."

"What has caused mankind to dip into this toxic pig bath? Ghant Wackersham represents the lowest point in mud-wallowing history. Occasionally, a newsperson describes him as 'morally bankrupt.' But mom, that's not true. He never had any scruples to bankrupt. He was simply born without any willingness to determine right from wrong. And he has zero capacity to deal with human suffering. He ain't gonna win, anyway."

Mandy held her hands over her ears. Oliver continued, "Your son has grown up with enough sense to eschew such swindlers. Aren't you happy about that? Wackersham and the Conservaprick Party are natural-born bamboozlers!" Oliver paused and took a deep breath, looking up the weather on his smartphone. "Mom, all politicians suck."

The great Wilbert Noah Stokes once said something like, "The only rule I would have in my Libertarian democracy would be that the moment someone appears to aspire to political office is the moment you permanently ban them from politics! Period!"

"Let's just forget it," Mandy insisted, removing her hands from her ears.

"He's probably an Allcon too."

"Who?" asked Mandy. "Ghant Wackersham?"

"No, damnit. This Tug guy."

"Oh, Oliver. I wish you wouldn't. How did you know that?"

"Just a guess. "Well, I've told you about those fakes. They're not even real Gorebingerz! And real Gorebingerz are bad enough. But the Allcons—that's some made-up nonsense from the 1800s. They're in their own league of stupidity." Oliver petted Phoenix for a moment. Then, a more dreadful thought occurred to him. "Don't tell me he likes Elvis too?" he asked, dripping with sarcasm that even the incredible Blob couldn't absorb.

"I don't know, I haven't asked him yet," replied Mandy Jo. Oliver cringed whenever Mandy Jo played her sappy Elvis ballads. To him, Elvis was the most overrated musician ever. He would leave the house whenever Mandy Jo dug out her "glorified white hillbilly" CDs. "Oliver," she would say every time he criticized the American public's adoration of Elvis, "I think those reefer twigs make you crazy!"

"Mom, they're not twigs; they're buds."

"Well, whatever you call 'em."

The outspoken modern-day hippie took a giant bite out of his Harold Buttquick thin-sliced meat sandwich.

"Oliver," Mandy said, "I'll be damned if we don't disagree on everything. But son, I love you. Please don't be so harsh. One more thing. "Tug and I both like cheese puffs and professional wrestling."

"Well," said Oliver with a mouthful, "there's the root of all the fraud right there. Professional wrestling. And not only Tug, but Ghant Wackersham probably likes wrestling as well. That's why he's so good at being a fake."

"Now there you go again about Ghant!"

"Mom, he fornicates with harlots, conducts a scam shop, and doesn't even like animals. He has no pets! And he has no clue how to tell the truth! He makes Schmidt look like a priest. And just think—I'll have to pay this fucker's pension! No way."

They better not elect him, or I'm leaving the country!!!" Oliver again ripped into his sandwich. Then, with a mouthful, he said, "Oh, and he's the world's *worst* capitalist! Everything he touches turns to shit."

"Well," Mandy Jo reasoned, "what's wrong with being a capitalist?"

"Mom," explained Oliver, "capitalism was alright when it was just one-on-one bartering in the public square. But as soon as they invented The Corporation, everything went south."

"Well, what's wrong with going south?" Mandy wanted to know. "I like the south."

"Mom, it's just an expression. I mean everything went to hell. Anything that grows big under capitalist rule goes to hell. Companies, churches, any bus—."

"I like my church!" protested Mandy Jo.

"You don't even *go* to church!"

"Well, I still like it."

Post-Election Joy

"Hot Dog! We won!!!" said the meaty-limbed truck driver, pulling the sheet from his bedding.

Tug woke up to his radio-alarm clock's announcer jubilantly declaring that with a late-evening rally, Ghant Wackersham, the Conservaprick hero, had won the presidential election. Tug later celebrated by snuffing out another victim, leaving her in a Forest Preserve in Calumet City, Illinois. The thrill from Ghant's victory and the girl's demise sent exhilarating shivers down Tug's spine. As he choked her out, he felt a lifetime of troubles melt away from his mind. He had managed to glean that she had a liberal bent, and as he performed his rituals, he shouted, "I hate fucking Librhoids!"

Tug wanted so much to bathe her feet before removing her toenails, but he knew it would take too much time.

After dispatching his latest victim, he drove down Interstate 55, listening to "Ghant Rants" on his tape machine. About two hours into his trip to Rolla, Missouri, he stopped at Big Bill's Country Pantry on the west side of Blandon, Illinois.

An excited buzz dominated the atmosphere of the little glorified hick joint (for some of the last remaining hillbillies in town), as Tug munched on his eggs and bacon.

The place was packed full of Central Illinois Conservapricks. As Tug dug into his second helping from the buffet, a gentleman asked, "Is it OK to sit here?"

"That depends," responded Tug, "whether you voted for Ghant or not."

"Why, yes sir, I sure did."

"Go right ahead, partner," said Tug.

"Thank you."

"You'z guys out for Sunday breakfast?" asked Tug.

"Yes," answered Melvin Goodall, "but it's more like brunch."

Tug wondered what "brunch" was. Then, he said, "I'm headed for Missouri."

"Why, that's interesting," commented Melanie.

"My name's Tug. What about you?"

"Mel and Mel," replied Melanie with one of those certified, fabricated real-estate-agent smiles.

"You're both Mel?" Tug let go of a big hearty chuckle.

"He's Melvin, and I'm Melanie," explained a tickled Melanie.

"So, where else do you go, Tug?" asked Melvin.

"Aw, I travel all over the Midwest. Missouri, Arkansas, Indiana, Ohio, you name it. Here's one of my cards."

Melvin took the card, glanced at it, and inserted it into his shirt pocket behind the pen and tiny notebook he always carried with him. "Nice," he said. "We're just celebrating Ghant's victory today."

"Damn tootin'!" exclaimed Tug. "It's a gift from God."

"Praise the Lord!" responded Melanie.

"I voted yesterday morning up near Chicago," Tug reported. "We're gonna take it to those damn Librhoids!"

"Oh yes," added Melanie, "we're so excited! This is like the second coming of Gore," she said, pulling out her little Ghant! button and pinning it to her blouse. "The world is a different place today."

Just then, Melanie noticed a man sitting at the next table. He had a large tattoo on his forearm—a skull with a joint in its teeth and smoke pouring out of the cavity where the nose would be. "That's sinful," Melanie blurted out, pointing at the man's arm when he looked her way. The guy smiled and turned away. Melanie then turned her smile toward Tug, and the horny trucker thought dark thoughts about her and her arrogant grin. Indeed, Melanie's beauty and confidence made a strong impression on the murderous road hauler. Her sharp features, small nose, and full lips made her an attraction to any man, sane or insane. Tug imagined what Melanie's eyeballs would look like on sticks. He almost reached orgasm right there at that little table when he thought about injecting the douche solution into her moist vagina.

Double Doing

Elma Ray was a somewhat heavy-set black woman with a heart of pure polished pearl. She bought—even though she could scarcely afford it—extra canned food at Floor-Mart to help the homeless and even a few of Sparky's Paradise Inn's tenants. She appeared so friendly and earnest to the bank officials foreclosing on her home that they agreed to a deal allowing her to stay and pay less on a temporary basis. With no bitterness toward the Indians of the East, she carried on with confidence, believing she would find a good job soon.

Meanwhile, Tyrel thrived with his music, starting a band of mixed-race musicians. The guitar player was Jason Stockwell, an Anglo-Saxon kid from West Springfield. The bass player was Hernando Vargas from the Central District, of Mexican descent. On violin was Ton Watanabe, a Japanese-American kid with the highest musical IQ of the group. And the keyboard player was Tony Maranto, whose parents were Italian immigrants. They practiced feverishly in the basement of Elma's house. Elma felt good about providing the band with practice space, allowing her to keep a close eye on Tyrel. Despite the challenging times, she refused to deny her son a pleasant and meaningful childhood, even as she kept her own troubles hidden.

So, when Elma privately held her right hand over her chest and pledged "I will provide a good home for my son," she repeated the same with her left hand.

Elma worked very hard at her motel job. "You don't have to make the sinks so sparkling clean, Elma," cautioned Timothy "Sparky" Gleason, the motel owner. "This ain't the Hilton."

"Yes, Mr. Gleason," Elma responded, knowing full well that, yes, they *have* to be sparkling clean. And, yes, I'm going to vacuum every morsel of this or that from the carpet. And, yes, the bedsheets must be made in perfect, symmetrical order. Yes, I must fold the shredded end of the toilet paper just like they do at the Conrad Hilton. And, yes, I will scrub the bathroom and kitchenette floors on my hands and knees, even if it means staying on my own time to do it!

True, Sparky's was the dumpiest motel in the cherished Blandon-Average metro area, but even its worst was a couple of levels above the worst elsewhere. The people of Blandon act a little uppity, thought Elma. They don't stoop to drink from fountains but sip from tiny cups from dispensers next to each fountain. Their playgrounds don't have monkey bars or merry-go-rounds; instead, they have tennis courts, pickleball courts, and shuffleboard tables. And everyone drives an oversized Sport Utility Vehicle, plays golf, and roots for the Chicago Cubs.

Finally, Blandon became the first place you would ever see a Conservaprick long-hair, but that was back in the 1980s. Nonetheless, it was a deflating sight to Oliver Rhodes' psyche.

Oliver once told another student, "I always got the impression from Blandon-Average people on the east side of town that they were hatched from pods out in the cornfields that surround the place. They were indeed like plants. Not much character, not much culture, beyond what the many stuffy evening spots offer. The people live in a bubble. The fancy restaurants of Bubbledumb help perpetuate this pod culture. And the local newspaper, which Oliver called the *Plant Rag*, ensured that the residents of Bubbledumb remained ignorant of Conservaprick malfeasance and kept their carefully crafted bubble impenetrable.

One rainy evening, Elma discussed world issues over the phone with her friend Maria Santos, who was now working as a hostess at Frederick's, one of Blandon-Average's many yuppie and well-heeled dining establishments.

"Oh my God, Elma," Maria said, "he won! I can't believe it. For crying out loud, what has America become?"

"I don't know, Maria," Elma responded. "It's a great big mess. And they think he's a genius."

"I have this liberal friend at work," Maria explained, "and he said, 'Wackersham is a veritable sleazeball.' But those Conservapricks just love him."

"Yes, they do, Maria."

"Oh Elma, what are we going to do? It's a growing disease, like Covid and the pandemic."

"I don't know, dear," said Elma, "just go on with our lives, I suppose. Hopefully, he can't do too much harm. I mean, hopefully, Congress will block him from becoming a dictator." A long pause brought stress upon both ends of the conversation, before Maria changed the topic.

"Did you read the paper today?" asked Maria.

"No," replied Elma, "I've been so busy that I haven't even had a chance to hear or read any news today."

"They think we might have a serial killer here in Central Illinois."

"Oh, my goodness, that's terrible news."

"They have found three bodies that they think are all related," said Maria.

"How are they being killed?" asked Elma.

"By strangulation."

"Oh dear, I'll have to take extra precautions," said Elma.

"Don't go out alone at night, Elma. That's the main thing. Just make sure you are with somebody."

"Thanks, dear," said Elma, "I'll watch the 10 o'clock news tonight."

Somewhere amongst the towering rows of corn and the twinkling rural porchlights, Tug, himself, listened to the news about him on the radio. "That's right, daddy," he bragged, "I choke 'em and plug 'em."

A Grim Affair: Post-Election Gloom

"Now a word from our new Chief Executive, President Ghant Wackersham," a voice on the television announced. And there he was, sitting in the Oval Office as if he had earned it on merit, and not stupidity.

"Friends, comrades, this afternoon we embark on a new and exciting chapter in American political history—a chapter steeped in order and control. We will dismantle the sinister liberal machine, piece by piece, until the wheels literally fall off. This is a chapter where the scandalous views of the dithering liberal will be obliterated. And with this evil machine will go the nefarious Librhoid Party members who have made life so easy for loafers and invaders, and so miserable for the honorable Conservapricks."

Wackersham cleared his throat and tapped the microphone like an imbecile. "Gone are the shit-laced mechanisms by which immigrants gain admittance to this nation and build power. I vow that we will take back our nation and make America wholesome once again. That's all I have for now."

But the outline of our program will soon emerge. Let the liberal bastards flee and hide. The new regime for a better and cleaner America has arrived. Thank you and God bless you all."

•••

Depression had settled into Oliver's soul like a thick fog blanketing the ground. He thought to himself, only morons could have voted for such a big-mouthed miscreant as Ghant Wackersham, yet just over half the voting population adored him. What kind of mass mental illness had gripped the population? Would democracy survive? They should have tried President (it irks me to even think of him as President) Schmidt for orchestrating an insurrection; then they wouldn't be stuck with this Wackersham mess.

"Mom," cried Oliver, "he goes on terrifying tirades and whips people into a veritable frenzy. The papers call him a 'demagogue.' He is a bona fide swindler. So why do his followers adore him so much? It's a twisted adulation for a bellicose madman."

"A 'bella' what?"

"Mom, he's a sociopath and probably a sadist. He is for sure the greatest magician ever to occupy the Oval Office. Don't you see? He's pulling the wool over America's collective eyes."

"Now Oliver," reprimanded Mandy Jo, "he's our president. And I won't have you disrespecting him."

"Is *that* what you want representing you around the world?"

"I'll have no more of it, Mister!"

Oliver begrudgingly retreated to his room to study. He had two upcoming tests in his college coursework, and he had to work the next four nights at The Happy Hamburger. He wanted so badly to be on his own, but he knew he was still needing his mother's support while going to school.

"And Oliver, I wish you'd quit talking over my head. You know I only made it to the eighth grade."

Oliver shut the bedroom door and lay down on his bed with his book, *Theories in Discourse*. He read for a while before drifting into an uneasy slumber. In his dream, he floated aimlessly above a dome of fluffy clouds, feeling frustrated by his lack of control over his direction. Suddenly, the phone rang. Startled, Oliver rose and answered it. It was his girlfriend, Lisa Westman.

"Hello Oliver," she sighed. "I'm sure you heard the bad news."

"Yep. We're doomed."

Lisa came from Forest Heights, a ritzy subdivision of West Springfield. She was a pretty, Thronez Librhoid whose parents were staunch supporters of the new President.

"I didn't think there were enough crazies to elect him," said Oliver. "Boy was I wrong."

"Well dear," Lisa suggested, "most Americans were wrong. I think I'll disown my parents."

"Yeah, I think I'll disown my mom."

"If the Librhoid Party hadn't put up such a bad alternative candidate, we would have won. America will never be the same."

"Well," Oliver explained, "ever since the Librhoids aligned with the Irad War of Lies, things haven't been the same. I mean, we couldn't even react when Russia invaded Ukraine, considering we had done something similar to Iraq just twenty years ago."

"I know."

"It's like a mass PTSD situation, maybe triggered by the events of 9/11. Half the population seems to have lost their grip on reality. It's as if they've lost the ability to reason. What exactly do they expect from this guy—this swindling, diabolical freak—this corporate-friendly elitist?"

"I know, dear. Sorry."

"Sorry?" Oliver chuckled, "it's not your fault, Lisa."

"I know, but I feel so helpless."

"Are you comin' over tonight?"

"Yes," answered Lisa, "I just have to do a few things at the Homeless Shelter, then I'll be coming over. I'll see you at 7 o'clock. Love you."

"Love you too. Bye."

So, the hours of that dismal day dragged on, shrouded in darkness and uncertainty, leaving a tumultuous mix of highs and lows across the Western Hemisphere.

Oliver picked up his Economics book, flipped it open to a bookmarked page, and began to read. Within thirty seconds, he tossed the book aside and pondered his place in the universe. He thought: The capitalists try to present their ideas with dry terminology, charts, and numbers, but it's just a pathetic sales pitch. America is swarming with salespeople. That's not science. Whether they're selling you a shirt, a garden tool, or trying to impress their views on you, it's all part of the sales game. It has so pervaded American life that, whether we like it or not, we all suffer from what I'd call Obsessive-Manipulative Disorder. We can't find happiness unless we're selling something. We either beg or trick you into buying something—whether abstract or material—and that's capitalism boiled down to a kernel of popcorn.

Then Oliver said aloud: "I'm so sick of reading and hearing about economies of scale, profit margins and demand curves, I could puke right here. If anyone ever asks me for a work-breakdown structure, I'll just haul off and vomit right in their face."

"Oliver," cried Mandy Jo from the other room, "who are you talking to?"

"No one, mom. Just talking to myself."

Suddenly, the phone rang. It was Oliver's boss at Happy Hamburger. "Hello, Oliver?"

"Yes."

"This is Donna Gustafson. Can you work tonight? I have two call-offs and I need you badly."

"What time?" asked Oliver.

"From 5:00 to close. Can you do it?"

"Yes, I'll see you at five."

"Oh, thank you, Oliver! Bye now."

Donna Gustafson was a fair boss but was deeply involved in the women's liberation movement. Oliver once saw her and her partner jogging through the park, and he was taken aback by the sight of Donna's unshaven armpits. Despite his initial shock, he quickly adjusted, having always supported gender equality. Donna had shared her family's history with him: her great-great-grandmother had been part of a team that pushed Congress to pass the 19th Amendment, granting women the right to vote. Her mother had also protested for women's rights in major cities like New York, Chicago, and L.A. Donna, though a tough manager at the hamburger stand, treated everyone with respect.

So, Oliver, the long-haired hippie throwback, admired her for that.

Returning to the living room, Oliver tuned in to the afternoon news, where the anchor reported on a serial killer on the loose in Illinois.

"Oh my God," said Mandy Jo, "I'm not going out at night anymore."

"Yeah," said Oliver, "but they said he kills by daylight too."

"Nobody's safe anymore," Mandy Jo reasoned.

"You never *were* safe in this world. Especially in America, where obvious mental illness dwells in half the population." Finally, the news anchor moved on to another topic. Oliver sighed and said, "There's a nut out there for everyone, Mom. He might not know you, and you might not know him, but somewhere your lives will intersect. Whether he's in a shooting mood when you meet him is another story. Yes, there's a nut out there for everyone. And the Conservapricks have put a gun in his hand."

"Do you have to make everything political?" Mandy Jo asked.

"And nowadays," Oliver continued, disregarding Mandy Jo's comment, "it could just as easily be a woman serial killer. Since women gained more rights," he added, quoting Mr. Westman, "they've become just like men—speed demons on the highways, adulteresses, and yes, even serial killers."

"They said he strangles his victims, Oliver."

So, it almost has to be a man. Women just aren't strong enough to do that. Besides, they said he kills prostitutes."

"Well," added Oliver, "perhaps you're safe then."

"I'm still gonna carry my pepper spray."

"He probably started out by torturing animals. But, oh well, we all torture animals."

"How so, dear?" asked Mandy Jo. "How do we torture?"

"Fishing." Mandy Jo was shocked. Oliver continued: "It's embraced as a family tradition. Dads take their sons and teach them. It's all part of the corny American values thing. Sometime in our lives, we have all tortured fish. And long ago, some hillbilly came up with the erroneous assumption that 'fish have no feeling.' At least not where you hook them, in their mouths."

AN EVENING WITH GHANT

"**I** used to do that stuff," admitted Tug. "I once took some Orange Barrel acid…back in the 80s."

"Wow," responded Candy. "I wish I had lived back then, especially during the 60s and 70s."

"Eh, It waren't so great," Tug declared. "Those damn hippies were full of shit."

"But I thought you said you had long hair."

"I did. But then I came to my senses."

With that, he grabbed Candy by the neck and squeezed like a boa constrictor. Just then, his cellphone rang. Holding Candy's throat tightly enough to silence her, he answered the call.

"Hello?"

"Tuggy, dear," said his mother on the other end, "did you remember to take your fiber bars before you left on your trip?"

"Mom, I'm kinda busy right now. Can you call me back? I'm on the job."

"I know, dear, but you have such problems going…"

"Mom, I'll call you back." With that, Tug ended the call.

As Candy drifted between consciousness and the brink of sleep, Tug pressed play on his tape player and wrapped a bungee cord tightly around her neck. The tape blared with the ranting campaign speech of Ghant Wackersham, Tug's latest idol.

"WE'VE GOT TO CHOKE THOSE LIBRHOIDS OFF AND SILENCE THE LIBERAL MEDIA!" Ghant's voice boomed. "OR ELSE WE'LL ALL END UP LIKE MISLEADING MALLORY [Mallory Winston, former President Schmidt's Librhoid opponent]. HOW DO WE DO THAT? IF YOU HEAR A LIBERAL ANNOUNCER, SHUT OFF YOUR DAMN TV! SHOULD YOU PICK UP THE PAPER AND SEE A LIBERAL WRITER, CRUMPLE IT UP AND THROW IT IN THE DAMN TRASH CAN! WHERE ALL THE LIBERALS BELONG!"

Just as Candy let out her final gasp, Tug cranked up the volume and, in a frenzy, ejaculated into his old bread bag. He grunted in ecstasy as he experienced a secondary orgasm. Breathing heavily and dripping with sweat, he released the bungee cord, overwhelmed by his exertions.

"I fucking hate dopeheads!" he screamed.

Then, he thought, I-57 had some nice wooded spots through Little Egypt. So, after a brief rest, he dragged Candy into the rim of the Shawnee National Forest in Southern Illinois. One of his rare trips down Interstate 57 found him on his way to Memphis, so the timing was ideal. Tug soon performed his eyeball, toenail and douche ritual with proficiency.

He returned to the truck and gloated over his cruel conquest and felt like a victory lap for old Ghant. Then, he mumbled something about wanting to change his routine. "Don't wanna be your average serial killer," he said out loud. "I've got to make changes. I can't go on this way. I have to use a different—what do they call it—mot--a motus, a motive, a modus oper—ration!"

Tug noticed a state cop passing as he was still rolling slowly on the shoulder of the interstate. Startled, he put on his turn signal, glanced at his side mirror, and steered the big rig onto the dark highway. He accelerated pensively.

Tug never hit, stabbed nor shot his victims in the truck cab. He wanted no blood evidence hanging around in his truck. In fact, once he did have to slug a wild prostitute who was too ornery to contain. He bloodied her well, and she dripped all over his carpet and console. He then let her go, telling her not to look at his license plate or he would kill her. With blood in his truck, he wanted no part of her death. As for Tug's DNA, should the law uncover it, he knew they would have no match. He was only in jail once for public intoxication, and that was well before they ever started collecting DNA.

"I want to kill someone who's *not* a prostitute," said Tug out loud. "That's it. Someone who's *not* a prostitute! Prostitutes are too fuckin' easy. I need a challenge!"

● ● ●

The physician introduced himself as Dr. Bannister. Patient and doctor shook hands.

"You are having some difficulty?" the doctor asked.

"Ah…yes." Answered Tug. "You see…when I…ejac—complete, well, I complete before I even penetrate."

"Yes," the doctor explained, "this condition is commonly known as 'premature ejaculation' in layman's terms, or *ejaculatio praecox* in scientific terms. It seems like a severe case, but you might be fortunate, as most men I see have the opposite issue: erectile dysfunction. That is, they struggle with getting and maintaining an erection. How long have you been experiencing this?"

Tug, not wanting to disclose that it had started around the time he began his killing spree, replied, "About three years," which was indeed the length of his killing spree. "Is there any treatment available?"

"There are several options. We can prescribe medication, provide you with penile exercises to do at home, or use various forms of stimulation to help with arousal, which you can then practice controlling ejaculation. We often use a combination of these methods for treatment. First, though, I need you to fill out a questionnaire."

"But doc," Tug protested, "the usual stimuli people use doesn't really work for me."

"We can work through it," the doctor said reassuringly, "if you'll just complete this paperwork."

"Just curious, doc, what's that drill used for?"

"That is not a drill, but a camera and scope. We insert that into the penis to look at the prostate and bladder." Tug's eyes grew large, as the thing was huge. "But don't worry, we will not have to use it in your case."

"I wouldn't let you use that thing on me, anyway. No offense, doc, but no thanks!"

"Have you ever suffered from a Sexually Transmitted Disease?"

"You mean," said Tug, "like a Venereal Disease?"

"Yes. Today, we call them STDs."

"OK. I get it."

"Are you experiencing pain in the groin area?

"No."

"Well then, as I said, we will not have to use it in your case."

THE REVELATION

"What is it, Buttercup?" asked Melvin. "You've been awfully quiet lately."

"Oh, I'll be OK," said Melanie. "Just a little tired today. A lot of houses to sell, you know."

Melanie set to polishing one of their $1,000 vases.

"No dear, there is something else bothering you. Selling houses never upset you before, not even during Spring rush, so what is it?"

"Well...."

"Is it me? You're not falling out of love with me, I hope."

"Well noooo. You're still my peach, my Master. I just—"

"What?"

"I've always wondered what it would be like…."

"Like what, buttercup? Like what?"

"Like—I better not."

"Say it!"

"What it would be like with a woman. There, I said it."

Melvin was taken aback. "A woman?" he echoed, clearly surprised. "How long have you been thinking about this?"

"Mmmm. A couple of years, maybe."

"Well, I'm baffled."

"There. I told you I shouldn't have said anything."

The chimes on the front porch rang softly, their solemn tones carried by the gentle breeze. The misty day seemed to amplify their melancholic melody, as if the damp air gave the bells a touch of blues. Melanie, always one to shy away from gloomy weather, found herself staring at her reflection in the sparkling glass of the $2,000 end table. The lamp illuminated her heavily made-up face, to the point where she barely recognized herself. The silence that followed was almost deafening. With a deep sigh, Melvin finally broke it.

"Well, my little Tulip, I suppose I wouldn't mind as long as…."

"Oh honey," blurted Melanie, "I still love you so."

"As long as it wouldn't be permanent or anything." Melvin paused. "I mean this would have to be a complete secret. I mean the church would never forgive us for that."

"Oh," exclaimed Melanie, "Forget I ever mentioned it, dear. It was a really silly thought."

"But I wouldn't know how to go about it. I don't—"

"Well," said Melanie, "Maybe you could think about it, dear. But right now, I would like you to make precious love to me."

"Oh Buttercup, you mean that?"

"My passion for you, Melvin, is overflowing." The pair of Spongez went at it harder and heavier than ever before. Melvin felt that he had to demonstrate his masculinity all over again, and Melanie thought about a feminine partner as they rolled and tumbled beneath those $800 silk sheets. It was a joyous occasion and a celebration of happy times.

•••

A week later, the righteous couple arrived in Hawaii for what they hoped would be a luxurious getaway.

Upon landing, they were greeted by the sight of a lively rally where native Hawaiians were celebrating their heritage and protesting American influence.

"Can you believe it?" Melvin remarked, a hint of disbelief in his voice. "Those native Hawaiians protesting against American rule?"

"They certainly have some nerve," Melanie agreed, her tone incredulous.

"They should be grateful for what the white race has done for them," Melvin continued. "They'd still be cracking coconuts if it weren't for us. Just look at the progress we've made."

"They're just a bit ungrateful, don't you think?" Melanie added.

"Yes," Melvin said, shaking his head. "They remind me of the American Indians. Just ungrateful savages."

The rest of their vacation proceeded without incident, and the renewed couple looked forward to retaking their wedding vows upon returning to Blandon-Average in the heart of Illinois. In their view, indulgence knew no bounds in the privileged enclave of Blandon's East Side.

RED MAWA CAPS

"What gets me," said Elma, on a phone call with her friend, Maria, "is that those Conservapricks always act like such goody-two-shoes and then they turn around and elect someone of such despicable character."

"Yes," cried Maria, "can you imagine if he was a Librhoid? What they'd be saying about us? Why, we would never hear the end of it!"

"Well, Maria, we'll just have to live with him for a while."

"But he's such a liar and a storyteller. How did we ever get to this place?"

"Oh, Maria, Tyrel just came in. Can I call you back?"

"Sure, hon'. I'll be home all night. Bye now."

"Bye-bye."

Elma hung up the phone and turned on the television. The evening news broadcast was "In Full Swing", and a clip of a Ghant Wackersham protest rally dominated the screen. The Librhoids were marching with fervor up and down the steps of the State Capitol in Springfield, and the footage even showed demonstrators gathering in Washington D.C.

"Tyrel! Dinner's almost ready! Did you have a good day at school?"

"It was OK," Tyrel answered, "What's for dinner?"

"Hamburger Helper!"

"Some bullies tried to make me wear a red 'Make America White Again' cap."

"They did what? Which bullies?" Elma demanded. "You mean one of those ugly red Ghant Wackersham hats?" She was furious. "I'll report them to the school. Do you know any of their names?"

"No, they were older guys."

"Here it is, 2028, and they're still pulling that crap!"

"Mom, can we have band practice tomorrow after school?"

"Did you clean up your room like I told you? Well, I suppose. But you must do your homework before practice…and without whining about it."

"Huh? I won't whine, I promise. Mom, could I get my own cell phone?"

"We can't afford it right now, sweetheart, but maybe soon…when Mom gets a better job."

"Is it true we're the laughing stock of the world now?"

"What?" asked Elma. "Who's the laughing stock?"

"America."

"Who told you that? Well, I guess those of us who aren't afraid are laughing…."

"Are you afraid, Mom?"

"I'm afraid that the Librhoid Party has lost the blue-collar vote, son."

"What's blue-collar?"

"It's the working people. The people who work in mills, warehouses, and stores, the people who drive trucks and taxis, as opposed to office workers. You know, the people who generally don't have college degrees."

"But you have a college degree, Mom."

"I know, sweetheart. But I'm wondering why it's not helping me right now."

CELLPHONE DISENGAGEMENT

As Oliver walked through Hyatt Park on his way home from Walt's Records and CDs, he passed by a small group of girls—who must have been fourteen- to sixteen-year-olds—and quickly noticed that one of the girls was having a tantrum, screaming and crying about something. Oliver asked another girl if everything was okay, and she told him, "Natalie is having a conniption over her broken cellphone." Oliver decided to focus on his own issues and said, "OK, just checking. Hope she gets a new one soon." He walked away with an uneasy, disturbed feeling. How someone could get so wrapped up in a small plastic box mystified him as he continued on his way home. He thought about the cellphone obsession and found it a silly addiction. People didn't even have cellphones thirty years ago, he thought. Never a big cellphone user himself, he vacillated between feeling sorry for the girl and being utterly amazed by her reaction. I guess the world has simply passed me by, he thought.

Later that week, Oliver noticed how many cellphone carriers' television and radio commercials intruded on his life. He told his friend, Jamelle, how disappointed he was with America's cellphone-crazy population. Then, still later that week, to Oliver's shock, he received a call from Ghant Wackersham's fundraising Campaign Committee of Central Illinois! "How dare you call me with this nonsense! I wouldn't give that scuzzy bastard the gum off the bottom of my shoe! Why don't you find something useful to do instead of campaigning for that Olympic-sized fraud! MORON!!!" With that, he hung up. How did those Conservaprick sleazeballs get my number? he wondered. I'm practically the biggest liberal on the planet!

"I hate politics," he later told Jamelle. "Always have. It's just that they forced this putrid Wackersham character upon me, so now I have to talk politics to help repel the bastard."

One day, after a flurry of garbage calls, Oliver, disgusted with an American public that clings to its cellphones like a dying grasshopper hugs a weed and ignores the alarm bells of what he interpreted as a fading democracy, took out his cellphone and hurled it against the sidewalk where it burst into a hundred or more pieces.

"That's it," he shouted. "I'm living without that fucking thing!"

"Dude," said Jamelle, "I don't believe you just did that!"

"I've had it with this stupid country and its distracted dimwits," stated Oliver. Then, to calm himself, he opened the front door, picked up Phoenix, and walked out to his mom's car. "Come on," he told Jamelle, while setting Phoenix in the front seat of the car, "Let's go for a ride."

The three of them rode off toward Ray's Roundup Restaurant, Phoenix sitting on Oliver's lap and looking out the window like a dog would do. "You know," said Oliver, "you could drop me in a forest, and I would find a way to entertain myself. I don't need any damn cellphone." When they pulled into the parking lot of Ray's, they saw a group of friends hanging out in front of the facility. Oliver parked close to the front door, and several of the group strolled toward the car. Josh Covington, one of Oliver and Jamelle's friends, sported a brand-new red Ghant! button. Oliver's stomach churned. "You're a Wackersham fan now?" he asked.

"Yeah, I think Wackersham's right for the country at this point," Josh answered. Noticing his friend's shocked demeanor, Josh apologized, "Sorry, pal."

A saddened Oliver stroked the fur of Phoenix and just looked down. He felt a sudden disconnection with Josh and grew afraid to inquire about anyone else's political leanings.

FRONTIER CONFEDERATES

Tug waded through a cluster of comments at the conclusion of an internet article on a hard-core conservative website. The piece was an editorial extremist rant on removing Librhoids from the politiscape. Tug participated by adding the comment, "Let's roll a Librhoid today!"

Almost immediately, someone responded to his comment by posting, "Our organization has interest in your philosophy. Please call xxx-xxxx for details."

Feeling bored and lonely, Tug decided to call the number. The person who answered invited him to a "secret meeting" the following night. The rendezvous would take place in an old farmhouse on the edge of a cornfield in South-Central Illinois. "Use the password, 'purge,'" declared the solemn voice on the phone.

The next night, Tug tucked his gun in his waistband and headed out into the sticks. He traveled way out on US Route 50, then, after a series of turns and a long stretch of gravel roadway, he spied the meeting place. He pulled into the lot, where a large Gambrel Barn housed what the recruiter called "the most decorated band of far-right conservatives in the nation." The faded red barn was nestled in a line of trees that broke a vast plain of corn and soybean fields.

He tapped on the big oak door, and a gentleman by the code name "Thor" answered. "Password?" said Thor. Tug replied, "purge," and the tall, gaunt man let him into a dust-caked interior with a circle of rectangular hay bales for seats. The sharp-featured host seated Tug on one of the hay bales and returned to his place by the door. The usual assortment of barn objects draped the walls of the wooden structure: wagon wheels, antique gardening utensils, horsewhips, and a few bumpers and other motor car parts. The seats filled up, and the meeting commenced.

Tug and a couple of other new members were introduced to the philosophy, motto, and customs of the secret society. They clearly understood that the group's cause was to promote Anglo-American values and strive for a "clean", white society. Ghant Wackersham had clearly earned his way into their embrace.

The morning stood dark and young before the meeting let out; Tug had begun his indoctrination as a "prospect" and went home to digest his new affiliation and its concerns.

Three months and several victims later, Tug underwent the grueling initiation experience and discovered the real mission of the secret society. First, they poured a bucket of "toad piss" over his head. Then, "The Father of Truth," a mysterious, sinewy figure with a pointed chin, shadows beneath his eyes, and a thick, black beard, made a sales pitch for their ideas on relieving the region, and ultimately, the entire country, of its Librhoid populace.

It seemed that Tug was the only surviving member of the new "prospects." The others had either been expelled or had gotten scared off. The main, long-term scheme of the extremist group, Tug soon learned, was to extinguish the blacks and the Quasars, but "only after they first extinguished the white liberals who enabled the blacks and Quasars." "You mean *kill* the white liberals first?" asked Tug, his hair soaked in smelly toad piss.

"We request that our brother not use such harsh descriptors and agree to our terms," pressed "The Father of Truth," "so that he can become a full-fledged member of our critical movement. 'Cleanse, Cleanse, Cleanse' shall be your mantra."

"This will not be another doomed, Manson race war," noted one ardent scholar of the philosophy, "but a gradual, methodical displacement and genocide." His long brow made shadows of his mysterious eyes.

"We cannot expect to eliminate blacks and Quasars," said The Father of Truth, "until we first rid the country of white sympathizers of the minorities. The enablers, that is, those who tout equality, whose ancestors ran the shameful Underground Railroad during the days of servitude, prosecuted the Quasar death-camp purveyors during the days of vengeance, and allowed Quasar to become a State, writhe and wiggle on our cutting board. Eliminating them is the initial order of business. Now, let us put them out of their own agony."

The man with the long brows warned, "We've heard the various rantings of the Anglo-Saxon warriors, the other so-called 'hate groups,' and we have concluded that their plans of purging the cities and countryside of the minority plague are either scattered efforts, weak, or altogether unrealistic. Our way is the only way. We have to purge the white enablers first."

The Father of Truth then explained, "To deliver this once-great land back to the white, ruling Confederate forefathers, let our plan rise to the top and never sink again. The Klu Klux Klan fell short of our target, and so did other secret patriots, such as the Oaf Weepers and the Skinheads." He paused with serious concern. "Clearly, we need more members, more actors to accomplish our goal of a clean Anglo society. But we must start slowly with random eliminations."

"It is ridiculous," said the long-browed man, "to think that we can clean up the country, dispose of the African and Quasari scourge, without first addressing the white enablers. This membership drive is to do just that. We need your assistance, Brother McRae. In the meantime, we are strengthening our affiliations with the hardest core of the militia groups."

"I'm surely crazy," later admitted Tug, "but I'm not *that* crazy."

Tug went along with the program of that day, but he never attended another meeting with the excessive, stern group.

Bundles of letters and emails soon clogged Tug's communication channels with messages begging his re-commitment to the hyper-critical group, and, later warning him to keep silent the things he had learned about the group. But Tug was "his own man." He refrained from the need to follow others. He went back to his lonesome solo operation.

A SAVAGE BLOW

Both Elma and Tyrel suffered through a difficult Saturday afternoon. Elma overslept and reported to work a bit tardy. Sparky did not say anything about it, as he knew of Elma's gleaming work record, but the already agitated motel maid started the day behind schedule, requiring her to toil hard to catch up.

Around 2:00 p.m., Sparky found it necessary to evict a rowdy, non-paying motel guest who was intoxicated on both alcohol and methamphetamine. Elma was busy changing the vacuum cleaner bag near the front desk when the manager and the intoxicated man approached. She had laid the overstuffed bag on the floor next to the vacuum. As the high and bitter evictee reached Elma, he kicked the full bag of dirt into the air, causing it to explode into a giant cloud of dust. Elma stood with her hands on her hips and a scowl on her face but said nothing. This created extra work for Elma, but at least Sparky had the front desk person call the cops, and in a few minutes, they hauled the hopped-up idiot to jail.

Meanwhile, Tyrel's experience was a lot more haunting in its gruesomeness and severity. Already quite upset at having to attend a classmate's wake, the young musician heard some commotion outside the funeral home. He stepped outside and saw a small crowd around the curb of the busy street. He quickly concluded that it was a highway accident. As he approached the scene, he realized a pedestrian had been struck by an automobile. Tyrel squeezed through the crowd and saw what he thought was a fifteen- or sixteen-year-old boy lying on the pavement with his arm and coat over his face. One of the startled but nosy onlookers lifted the boy's coat to expose his face, and to everyone's horror, a stream of blood from the victim's nose and mouth ran to the curb. An ever-widening puddle of blood formed as the crowd shrank away in terror. The boy coughed up more blood as the onlooker let go of the coat and moaned, "Oh, my God."

An approaching ambulance drowned out the coughing and spitting up of blood from the poor youth. Everyone knew it would be a Herculean task to keep him alive.

Tyrel returned home that day in a daze of worry and confusion.

When he met his mother at the door, he hugged her tightly—more tightly than ever before.

Immediately sensing that something was wrong, Elma said, "What is it son? Are you OK?"

"I witnessed a terrible thing, mother, just a terrible thing," the boy said.

"Aw, well come in and tell your mother all about it, dear," responded Elma with caressing hands. She listened to her son's detailed description of the harrowing incident, and her own worries seemed to fade away like a rapidly dissipating cloud of steam beneath a baking sun. Tyrel felt worthless the rest of the evening. He tried to do homework, but failed to concentrate. He tried to practice syncopation on his rubber practice pad, but could not even keep time with the metronome.

The next day, Tyrel and his mother learned that the boy had, indeed, passed on. Tyrel's already battered heart absorbed another vicious blow. For at least a week, thereafter, he could not wrestle his thoughts away from the emotionally exhaustive experience.

PENNY FOR A PAUPER

The Two Mels raced up Interstate 55 in their 2028 Lincoln Navigator, a luxury SUV with three rows of plush seats, only two of which they utilized, one for their luggage and another for their bodies. They were headed to Orchestra Hall in the Symphony Center on Michigan Avenue in downtown Chicago, just blocks from The Magnificent Mile, where Melanie loved to shop for overpriced merchandise and mingle with the Windy City's upper-class go-getters. They planned to enjoy a fall concert with the Chicago Symphony Orchestra performing Mozart favorites, sleep in a luxurious hotel, and then shop the following morning.

Melanie, no debutante, had frequented the corridors of The Loop many times before, her Botox-swollen 33-year-old face a familiar sight. Her colorful lips, cheeks, and eyelids, resembling Halloween makeup, testified to her extensive experience in modeling lipstick, rouge, and eye shadow in generous applications.

The two lovebirds soon slipped onto Lake Shore Drive, zipped up to a Michigan Avenue parking garage, and walked to the Symphony Center. Just before entering the concert hall, Melvin noticed a presumably homeless man seated on the cool concrete sidewalk near the entrance of the stately building. With over-acted drama and a showoff manner, the cash-fat financial advisor tossed a single penny into an empty collection canister where it rang like an overused cowbell. Before the panhandling tramp could even slip Melvin a dirty look, the smug smartass ducked into the lobby of the hall.

The Two Mels thoroughly enjoyed the show, as did the rest of the audience, rising from their seats with a standing ovation. The couple only needed to stroll to the Drury Inn to celebrate an evening of vitality and sparkle. They would soon sip fine wine and partake in filet mignon, before retiring for a quiet night of elegant comfort.

But when they walked outside of the music hall, the beggar from earlier in the evening saw Melvin. He slowly got to his feet and approached the affluent pair. Suddenly, he pulled a pocket knife from his tattered coat, lunged at Melvin, and stabbed him in the back.

"You beady-eyed Devil!" yelled the assaulter. Then, as if nothing had happened, he went and sat down in the same place. Meanwhile, Melvin had collapsed onto the dull concrete, where he rolled onto his side and groped at the fresh wound.

Fortunately, the wound was up near the shoulder blade and away from the heart. Soon, Melvin was whisked away in an ambulance and the bold panhandler arrested. Melvin spent the night in the hospital, eating macaroni and processed turkey, while Melanie dove into her steak at the plush hotel. Before leaving for home the next morning, the couple learned that the panhandler was a known schizophrenic. Melvin never revealed to anybody, including Melanie, that he had in some way provoked the attack.

LGBTQ IN THE PARK

Oliver meandered through the old downtown Springfield, where 19th-century Romanesque Revival architecture clashed with a few modern buildings. Soon he heard a loudspeaker broadcasting a voice of strength and defiance. As he followed the sound, he began to notice many odd people hanging around a small park. Women dressed as men; men dressed as women; flamboyant creatures who looked like neither man nor woman. Soon he found himself in the midst of a freak fair, approaching a stage with an animated public speaker and a sizeable crowd that listened intently. A large sign read "LGBTQ Rally" and another read "Feminists Support the Queer Movement." Oliver could not tell if the speaker was a man or a woman, so he moseyed a bit closer. It was a woman speaker with short, cropped hair. She wore a muscle shirt and had hair hanging out from her armpits. She obviously had on a chest binder and wore military fatigues for trousers.

"The theologians will carry us back to the cradle, or worse," said the woman intensely. "Where man wields his cock like a thorny whipping stick and woman is relegated to a semen receptacle." Cheers sprang up from the enthusiastic audience.

"It's OK to question the Gorebingers," she continued amidst a short burst of cheers, "and the fairy tale book that transported them to imaginary glory!" Now the crowd cheered, jeered and whistled in a mix of emotions.

"Afterall," she cautioned, "religion is simply a device to perpetuate the elevation of man over woman." The crowd roared with rebellious zeal. "A tool to maintain female subservience."

Oliver stabbed at a couple of explanations for her hardcore presentation. Maybe she is the dominant half of a lesbian relationship, he wondered. Perhaps she is an Asexual...or a transgender person, guessed Oliver, staring at a screen behind her with her name on it. It was quite neutral: "Peyton Remy Stronghorne."

Peyton continued: "And whom do you think is the main purveyor of this antiquated belief system?" He or she paused a moment, while the crowd buzzed and milled about. "THE CONSERVAPRICK PARTY!" A seismic burst of emotion from the audience vibrated the eardrums. "Yes, the Ghant Wackersham regime tried to quash this rally, you know. That bunch of totalitarian plutocrats launched their attacks from every angle they could play. Ghant Wackersham, the King autocrat worm, tried his damnedest to thwart our movement. But he did not succeed!" Peyton peered out into the restless crowd. She continued: "And the Gorebinger-sponsored female servitude thing has got to stop!"

"Now," whispered Oliver, "Peyton is talking my dialect."

The crowd grew noticeably larger, once Wackersham was mentioned. Professional women and even housewife-types wandered in and gravitated toward the stage. Even a few men sauntered in, though Oliver did see one man who told his wife, as he backed away, "I ain't gonna be seen with these people. I'd never hear the end of it on the shop floor!" His wife was undisturbed by his fem-phobia but curious to hear more.

"I think I'm supposed to refer to Peyton as 'they,'" muttered Oliver. "I don't know…but I want to learn…."

Just then, an old man with a cane and a balding head came hobbling toward Oliver and said, "Boy, boy. Now ain't that just a shame. You cain't tell what they iz anymore, a boy or a girl. This whole bunch is headed to Perdition!"

Oliver glanced down toward the cracked sidewalk to hide his smirk. "Well," he explained, "it's the LGBTQ movement."

"The wha?" protested the scornful old man.

Oliver pointed toward the signs and said, "Lesbian, Gay, Bisexual, Transgender, Queer movement." Meanwhile, Peyton Remy Stronghorne ranted on about religion protracting the subservient-women fallacy.

"They's queer awright," he squawked. "They ain't fit to live, if yer askin' me."

"You see," explained Oliver, "I don't claim—er, pretend—to understand them, myself, sir. But you've got to admit, socially, we're way ahead of other countries. You can really learn something by listening to them."

"Sheeeit!"

"They do have rights, sir, even if they are a little forthright about it."

"God Damnedest thing I ever saw. They's just pitiful."

Oliver knew the old man was holding back. That he would like to tear that stage down and shoot everybody on it.

The old man spoke his final words. "The America I come from wouldna' put up with this trash." The indignant codger turned to walk away. "Teh!" he griped, while waving his hand.

Oliver could see him shaking with rage and disgust as he exited the park. The young hippie wanted to say one last thing, but the old guy had already left. He said it anyway. "The America *you* came from forced people to hide it. To conceal their identity." Oliver rubbed his chin. "New time. New country."

Oliver surprised himself that he had something good to say about America. He did notwant to be the disgruntled, defiant youth *all* of the time.

Amidst Oliver's exchange with the old man, a new speaker had taken the podium. It was Angela Rodriguez, a fiery, tough-looking woman with a dark complexion and jet-black hair. She pretty much yelled everything she said into the microphone. "The Gorebinger fundamentalists will transform America into an authoritative capitalist theocracy, if we let them! It's happening now! It's been happening! Ever since the Supreme Court Conservaprick's granted immunity to any criminal who shall hornswoggle his or her way into the Oval Office, it has been happening! On a gradual pace America has been sinking...slipping into tyranny! They have arrested a woman's right to terminate a pregnancy! Before it's over they'll have you kneeling at the feet of Gore Binger three to five times a day—mandatory! Whether you believe in him or not! Worse yet, they'll have us all kissing the toes of Wackersham!!!"

The crowd let out one heaving sigh. The whistlers started up and the entire crowdparticipated in a howling wall of noise.

"Ever notice how nature was assigned the female sex? Is that supposed to be because nature is often on the rag?" Another burst of crowd noise followed. "Frankly, I hate Mother Nature! I don't respect her! This fem fiend steals lives. It's where this capitalist 'Only-the-strong-shall-survive' bullshit came from!" Some people knew not what to make of Angela's rant. Perhaps, thought Oliver, she's gone off script. She continued: "Nature cloaks herself in all the beautiful forms and colors: green, red, yellow, purple, etc., while allowing animals to stalk and eat each other! Have you ever felt for the poor deer who succumbs under the tearing teeth and nails of a leopard? Mother Nature, I tell you, she's the planet's biggest phony too! And the dog-eat-dog madness of capitalism is patterned after this killer bitch!" Now the crowd went into an orgasmic frenzy, whooping and jeering at the stark revelation.

"Mother Nature! She let's children starve. She launches hurricanes that gobble-up buildings and innocent people—and even her own self—in the case of trees. Yes, she's a self-abuser! She rips out her own trees, for cryin' out loud! She begets fire and tornados that exterminate her own subjects. She unleashes tsunamis and earthquakes! It's not fair that nature was deemed a *she*, I tell you!"

The audience began to shrink a bit. But the vociferous ones were still present.

"Mother Nature has all the earmarks of a psychopath! A certified psychopath, I tell you! Fits of rage! Homicidal indifference! An arsonist! A sneaky spitball death peddler! She teams up with Fate and deals out death! She hurls floods and avalanches! All of this when she is on the rag! It was the male species who labeled nature a "mother!" It's disparaging! A frantic woman on the rag! That's all! Peace and love everybody!!!"

FLIGHT OF THE PHOENIX

"Here he is, Oliver!" announced a thrilled Mandy Jo. "Now be nice."

"I'm not going to say anything," assured Oliver. "He can't help that he's a Wackersham supporter. They're all retarded."

"Please."

And there he was, Tug McCrae, strutting up the sidewalk to the porch in a glaring red "Isolate America" T-shirt. Tap, tap, tap. Even his knocking grated on Oliver's nerves.

"Come on in!" Mandy invited cheerfully. She greeted Tug with a hearty hug. "Hi Tug!"

"Hello Mandy Jo. Great to see you!"

Right away, Phoenix disliked their guest. The cat scampered into the kitchen, arching his back, stretching, and sniffing his food dish before slinking off into a closet.

Tug was a towering figure, standing 6 feet, 3 inches tall with big, hairy arms, a slight pot belly, and lifeless eyes. His brown, messy hair peeked out from under a MAWA hat, and he sported a short, dark beard, mustache, and bushy eyebrows. His head was notably wide.

America's falling apart, Oliver thought as he stared at the hulking visitor. No matter how the media spins it, or how the Protectors of Legacy try to sugarcoat this disaster, we're in a national crisis. Look at this big, dumb hillbilly.

"And I suppose you're Oliver," the lumbering giant said with a hint of sarcasm, extending his large, calloused hand. Mandy Jo must have told him about Oliver's liberal views.

"Yep," Oliver replied. "Hey Tug."

Oliver was known for his sharp criticisms of the globalist movement, both in speech and writing. But "Isolate America"? Really? It's irrational, he thought. It's reactionary nonsense, spread by that colossal fool, Ghant Wackersham.

"Where are you from?" Oliver asked.

"Chicago area. Wheeling, Illinois."

Oliver immediately thought of the lame Urban Cowboy trend of the 1980s he had read about. Tug, he figured, reminded him of that bygone trend. Then he remembered Wilbert Noah

Stokes and his writings about the transplanted southern culture in the industrial north.

"You guys are from down yonder," Tug blurted out. "Springfield is beyond the sticks."

What a stupid thing to say, Oliver thought. This is the land of Lincoln. Far more progressive than Tug and his ignorant associates will ever be. Here's this guy who looks like an illiterate greaser hillbilly, telling me I'm from down yonder. What insipid drivel. What a paradox. What an overbearing ape.

"Well, Mandy Jo, I was thinkin' we could go up to McDonald's and have us a cheeseburger and a coke."

Then Tug's phone rang. "Hello," said the big man.

"Tuggy, stop by the house, dear. Mom picked up some donuts for you."

"Yes, mom," said Tug with total aggravation. "See you later," he said. Once he disconnected, he said in a low voice to no one in particular, "Mom, you ignored me when I was a kid. Now you pester me to death."

A red flag popped up in Oliver's mind. A neglected child, in his view, usually spells trouble later in life. This guy has to be watched, he thought.

Mandy Jo then asked, "Do you have a CD player?"

Tug answered, "Yes. You can bring any kind of music you like, as long as it ain't rap."

"What's wrong with rap?" asked Oliver.

"It's porch monkey shit," exclaimed Tug. "They brag about being criminals."

Oliver got defensive. "But hasn't 400 years of slavery and another 150 years of oppression earned them the right to be a little straightforward? A little audacious or even impudent?"

"I don't know those big words, but if you want to listen to spades shooting their big mouths off," reasoned Tug, "go right ahead. I just don't want any of it in my truck. I'll break it up and throw it out the window."

"Oh, jeez," sighed Oliver.

"Besides, things are gonna change now," snapped Tug.

"What do you mean by that?" asked Oliver.

"We ain't gonna allow them spooks to take over the country. And no Thronez either."

"You know," explained Oliver, "the Conservaprick Party is where all the racists go…and where all the political wackos go."

"Oliver!" cried Mandy Jo. "Don't."

"I mean every so often there pops up a leftist Librhoid wacko—like the guy who wanted to kidnap rich Spongez and drop them off in the ghetto at midnight and see if they can find their way out by morning—but most of the political extremist violence comes from conservative right-wing screwballs. Admittedly, that's a bit radical, but my point is that for every occasional liberal nut, there are 99 conservative nuts!"

"Well," replied Tug, "I don't know what these 'wings' are that you're talkin' about, but I know one thing: spooks aren't taking over!" He blurted this with emphasis, then turned around and looked out the front screen door toward the street.

"For Gore's Sake!" cried Mandy. "Please Oliver, just let it go! You know, Gore died for all of us. We have to get along. We must live together. In the name of Gore's sufferings...."

Mandy now floated into deep thought. She pictured in her mind the horrors of Gore. She imagined him being dragged to the Z Platform. He screamed, "I only meant that God could have some sensibility toward our female partners...that God might harbor some form of sensitivity in his constitution! Please! Please! Think what you are doing, my brothers and sisters!"

But the wicked-intentioned Thronez exhibited no mercy upon the wretched soul of Gore. His wrists and ankles were bound to the top and bottom of the Z-frame, respectively. He was then blindfolded. The Z was simply three logs carved into a flat surface and nailed together to form the shape of the last letter.

The Thronez then shoved red hot splinters beneath his fingernails. It was such a pain that no man has ever known. Poor Gore writhed with agony, hollering that he would someday rise up and revisit earth to lead his children to God's heavenly den in the azure sky. The unbearable pain became too much, as Gore's tortured syllables melted into a garble of meaningless grunts and moans—echoes from the sea bottom of mankind's primordial origin. "Aaaahhhh! Oh God, have mercy on my tormented soul! Agrhhhh! Abidy, abidy, abligordogrgleyehck!"

"You OK, mom?" asked Oliver, noticing a grimace on his mother's face.

"Oh, yes dear. Can't we please get along?"

Soon Tug and Mandy Jo were out the door.

Good riddance you numbskull, thought Oliver. I hope you trip over a parking block.

Oliver asked himself: "What brought on all of these far-right hate-mongers?" He wrote down his hypothesis and later read it to Lisa over the phone. "First of all, affirmative action pissed off the conservatives. They were not going to pay for the sins of their ancestors. Second, our diminished standard of living crept in, and I think people began to realize back in the 1990s that their standard of living might not be as good as that of their parents. No more convenient a group to blame exists than minorities and people of color. 'You have a lower standard of living,' the haters wrongly surmised, 'because of people of color and the Thronez, who own everything.' Then came along rap and hip-hop music. White supremacists cringed the moment they were exposed to the in-your-face style and its rhythmic blackness. They grew angry and lashed out at the audacity of the black man to rant about his sub-par condition. Finally, we have the Olson Presidency, the final blow to the militant groups and hate-mongers. A black president was just too much for them to digest. And there it is. That's how we got to this place."

"Very good," said Lisa, "and well thought out. Let us hope that this hatred dissipates over the years ahead."

"Yeah, it's 2029 and there's nowhere to turn at this point," moaned Oliver. "The Librhoid Party is weak and I never did forgive them anyway…for helping to vote us into the Irad War."

"I know, Oliver," said Lisa. "I tried to tell my parents, but they just would not listen. 'Mom,' I said, 'they lied us into a war with Irad!'"

"'Oh dear,' she said, 'don't say that.'"

"Can you at least admit they exaggerated?"

"'Oh hon', but the Conservapricks are heaven sent', she'd say."

"Yeah, I know," said Oliver. "My mom just shrugged when I told her what a garbage-brain Wackersham is. Then she said, 'Oh Oliver, Lord, all the other kids on the block grew up so normal. What happened to my son?'"

"If being 'normal' is voting for Wackersham," protested Lisa, "then you and I are hopelessly deviant…but proud of it!"

"That bunch up on the East Side of Blandon-Average—what does that make them?" Oliver answered himself. "A fat colony of those artificial vanilla ingrates, I would guess. They can be found in every well-to-do town, but not like the fakes up in B-A. They are in a class all by themselves."

"Wackersham's repugnance is astonishing," cried Lisa, "but the Blandon-Average elite just love him, don't they?"

THE GHANT RANT

"Are you ready to stomp some liberal butt?!" Ghant Wackersham shouted.

The crowd roared with misplaced enthusiasm. Their hero had triggered another riotous moment.

"The Librhoid Party will tell you that America's problems can all be solved with higher taxes, more lenient judges, and more illegal immigrants! What do you have to say to that?!"

The obedient crowd howled and booed, reaching a frenzied climax. The rabid jeers pained the eardrums of any decent member of the human race.

"Meanwhile, stocks are rising to unprecedented levels, unemployment is so low you could step over it, and everyone is sharing in the afterglow of economic goodness!"

Ghant! signs waved, and a sustained cheer echoed off the walls of this flimsy arena.

"What do you think will happen if the liberals vote in their man?!"

Another wicked surge in crowd noise distorted the television sound.

"I can't hear you?!" Wackersham taunted, cupping his hand to his ear.

The frantic but frustrated audience erupted into such feverish passion that the television sound cut out for a moment. It was just too much for the system to handle.

Finally, they quieted as Ghant raised his arm and leaned into the microphone. Suddenly, a lone liberal with a sign that read "Free Yourself from the Ghant Shackles!" shouted with as mighty a voice as one otherwise passive Librhoid could muster, "Down with fascism!!!" Again the crowd booed and hissed as a couple of Wackersham's henchmen dragged the overwhelmed heckler toward the exit. People started throwing cups and bottles at the guy and his liberal buddies, who followed him out of the arena.

"Slap the piss out of him, will ya?! I mean shut the bastard up!"

The crowd erupted into a massive, foul-mouthed tirade of unthinkable fury, smashing anything within reach, including chairs, tables, and even their own assembly-line fashioned Ghant! signs. The building shook with uninhibited rage. Outside the arena, the ill-willed Gorebingerz who escorted the liberal protesters out struck and kicked them, beat them with Ghant! signs, cursed them up and down, and otherwise mauled them like an over-stimulated pack of wolves would maul a chicken.

One of the protesters clung to his final breath, as the wolves re-entered the facility, not wanting to miss a word of Wackersham's sickening rant. Another protester had been stripped of his long hair, a clump of which the wolves had stuffed in his mouth. He wore a Peace belt buckle and a tie-dyed shirt. Spattered blood embellished the design. The sound of an ambulance approached.

"I mean so what if I sold a few documents to Russia? Sue me, goddamnit!"

The hideous crowd roared with demented pleasure.

"I remember the old days," croaked Ghant Wackersham, "when we were just a small, grassroots movement. When Oscar K. Schmidt sparked something inside you. When he called for the abolishment of the Washington D.C. political norm, he was a maverick. A true warrior rescuing an America that was fading in the wake of a black presidency. The unbridled fury of an electric audience stunned onlookers. The place was absolutely rumbling with madness.

"Yes, I remember those days. Schmidt was a special man, yet he still embodied a tinge of that Washington ilk, that machine that did what was expected. That 'Do things by the book' mentality. But, folks, we thrust that mentality out the window, out the porthole. And goddamnit, we're going to shape this thing the way we want it!"

A deafening ambuscade of grunts, "Yeahs," and other noises saturated the atmosphere like grape juice saturates a white tablecloth.

"Fuck rules!" yelled Wackersham, arms outstretched as if to gather all the anger in the room and harness it to his wicked platform of angst and hatred.

"I RULE!!! AND WHAT I SAY GOES!!! NOT THE WORDS OF SOME BLITHERING WASHINGTONITE! WE RULE!!! AND FUCK THEM ALL!!!"

As Oliver and Lisa watched this madness on their television screen, Oliver noted: "Just when you think his latest foul action will cause him to fall from grace, his popularity among the somnambulant fraud peddlers of the Conservaprick Party skyrockets."

"Yes, dear," said Lisa, "they want total control."

"Conservapricks have always had a streak of fascism in their party. They want—but will never get—total control." Oliver was fuming over the prickishness of the Wackersham warts. "The ultra-conservative freaks who run the party fought to ban alcohol in the 1910s, which gave impetus to organized crime in the form of bootlegging during Prohibition. "They would also like to ban marijuana. They, in fact, want to ban all vice, which would trigger a massive black market for just about everything. They tried to outlaw homosexuality. Next, they'll want to ban cursing. They resisted equal rights for blacks and women. They have their overwound assholes shut tight and want nothing to do with progressive thought. They would like to outlaw that too. They are mental dinosaurs. If you want to witness the real demise of Western Civilization, just let the Conservaprick Gorebingerz take over."

Lisa noted, "Wackersham encapsulates everything that was ever bad about capitalism."

"I'd vote for a turd in the sewer before I'd vote for him," Oliver remarked.

"He has no shame," added Lisa. "He overflows with venomous raunchiness!"

"That's right! With today's Americans, it's got to be more, more, more," said Oliver. "Got to have the biggest stereo speakers, the loudest car, the spiciest food. Pizza can no longer be just pizza. It's got to have loads of toppings, it's got to be dipped in sauce, and it's got to have a crust loaded with greasy stuffing! Stinky garlic-filled stuffing. And Ghant Wackersham has to be more offensive than anyone else on earth. Not just regular offensive, but so offensive that eating your own vomit would pale in comparison. Gluttonous Americans just can't get enough. It has got to be the pukiest version of a leader they can dig up!"

"Hey," said Lisa, "I like pizza."

"With all that shit on it?"

TUG THE REPUG

Tug wanted badly to quit picking up prostitutes at old motels, to quit calling them with numbers funneled to him by an unknown source, to quit murdering easy targets. "I've got to change my routine," he would whisper aloud, "so I don't get caught." For instance, he often thought about exterminating handsome, smiling couples like the ones shown on television commercials. "I need something more challenging. But how do I get my hands on them? How do I go about it?" Tug mused. Prostitutes made for such easy prey, and nobody gave a shit about them. "Must change…" he mumbled. "Got to do something different."

One evening, Tug picked up a date on Cicero Avenue in Chicago and drove her down to Tuscola, Illinois on Interstate 57 and US Route 45. He was on his way to Memphis and needed company. Just about to get a motel room, he was suddenly struck by an almost insatiable urge to kill. His victim was a cute little brunette with a thin face and lips—weathered, yes, but with a slim figure. He put the truck in park and immediately grabbed Paula by the hair, dragging her to the back of his cab. As he did, a wig came off Paula's head and Tug slapped his hand over her mouth and said, "I like short hair too, bitch!" He forced the petrified hooker into the back and flicked on his favorite Ghant Rant. "Well, I said I was bored. This one might be fun! Come on Pretty Paula...." He did his business, then carried Paula to a tiny forest behind the motel. But Tug was shocked to learn that this doomsday date was really a man. This he did not know until he pulled down the britches of the new corpse and commenced to inserting the douche. He fumed with the fury of a hell-sent lunatic. With ultra-rage he yelled like a tormented elephant. He yanked the snippers from his tool belt and whimpered while cutting the sack away with the two testicles still inside. "Little cocksucker!" he exclaimed. He then wiped the bloody snippers on his chemical suit and hung them back on his tool belt. Tug inhaled deeply and sighed in relief. But soon two glistening gonads rested atop a pair of sticks lodged in the dirt. He then beat the corpse with a hammer until he breathed heavily in the humid night air. The face was now unrecognizable. He ripped the billfold from the corpse's back pants pocket. "Paul Franco," read the big man. Only such an event could disgust the repugnant Tug. Finally, he slid a fresh douche up Paul's rectum and squeezed the bag with malice. Then he peeled off his chemical suit and retired back to his truck in despair. He was always looking for a way to change his game, and there he did it, even if it disgusted him and was by accident.

The next day, while the burly trucker was at his apartment, he did some heavy thinking. Lying in bed, he ruminated about his latest victim. He chuckled a bit and then looked up at his bedroom walls. They were lined with pictures of wrestling stars. Then there was the Wackersham Wall, "a monument to the man's genius," as Tug would say. Hundreds of photos of the demagogue ranting and hollering like the beloved lunatic he was. Rows of Ghant! posters and a couple of yard signs for his majesty. "God sent him to us!" Tug would declare to anything with ears. "A real honest to goodness Saint!"

GIBBY

"Hon'," said Melanie, "why do you suppose so many cops like Ghant?"

"Well, Buttercup," answered Melvin, "cops like control. They always want to have control of a situation. You see, Ghant represents that control to them. And under Ghant that is precisely what we have. Control. He is an inherent controller!"

"Oh hon'," blurted Melanie, "I almost forgot to tell you, I saw that colored guy…a client of yours…Mr. Gibson, at the grocery store today."

"Oh yeah? I like old Gibson. He talks like a white man, you know?"

"Yes, hon', he's quite articulate. Don't you wish more black people would be like him?"

"Why, yes Buttercup, I certainly do. Good ol' Gibby...."

As Pods of Bubbledumb, the Two Mels were a perfect pair. Either one could have hatched from a corn pod in a local field. Blandon-Average natives, they had both enjoyed exposure to shallow media, media that seldom revealed the scabs of the planet. When it did, it was only with a perfunctory glance. Not even a hint was given about the hyped-up case for the one-sided slaughter in Irad, which was treated as one of America's duties to clean up the world. Wackersham's perfidy was glazed over like a fresh, white doughnut. It seemed that the local media had a sole purpose of isolating and protecting the pods, ensuring they remained disconnected from the seedier side of society. As an outsider, Oliver had always surmised that the pods of the East Side of Blandon-Average were both "delicate and insulated." Their newspaper, *The Plant Rag*, maintained the bubble around the naive populace of Blandon-Average, especially flourishing on the East Side with its vapidity.

DIGGING FOR TRUTH

Elma wanted to network with people, so she started a Spacecrook page. Perhaps she could get a job tip from another user.

One night, though, after eight tough hours at the motel, she found herself immersed in a discussion about the Quasari-Pulsarian conflict in the Middle East.

"Learn about Quasar's oppression of Pulsarians," her Spacecrook friend, Fred, told her.

"Well," replied Elma, "I would certainly entertain the idea of learning more about the situation over there. But until then, I cannot make a judgement."

"It's a far-right thing," Fred wrote. "We in the West don't hear about the good people of Quasar who want equal treatment for the Pulsarians. We mostly hear about the ultra-conservatives who rule. Even the so-called liberal media here in America under-reports the mistreatment of Pulsarians and the opposition to the prevailing Quasari ruling party."

"Hmmm, I'll have to educate myself," Elma responded.

Then, one boneheaded user, "Captain Truth," posted: "Hell yes, Quasar is an Apartheid government. And the Thronez want to rule the entire Middle East, and after that, the entire planet. And they own the banking industry, and that's why you can't trust a Thronez!"

Elma was incensed by this type of behavior. She quickly wrote a rebuttal: "Here we are trying to have an adult discussion about a potential problem in today's world, and you go injecting racist strychnine into the matter. I don't have time or patience for stupidity. You'll have to post your poison elsewhere. Goodbye."

With that Elma immediately unfriended the bigoted Captain Truth, who, as far as Elma could tell, was full of no truth at all.

"Sorry," wrote Fred.

"Oh, you don't have to be sorry," replied Elma. "It's not your fault."

"Yes," wrote Fred, "those are the ones who are blurring the picture. We have to not get caught up in the hatred thing. We can't allow interference from guys like Captain Truth, or, should I say, Captain Crap. He's mucking up the waters of real truth and justice. We have to weed out the anti-Thronez. And when you peel away the layers of racism on all sides—Pulsarian, Quasari, or third-party Americans—you are left with a simpler problem that is definitely solvable. But Pulsarians need to quit using violence to deal with oppression and Quasaris need to halt the building of houses on occupied territory. That's a good thing you need to look up, Elma…'occupied territory.'"

OLIVER ON A ROLL

"I need to find out what the secret etchings are on the Allcon chamber pots," said Oliver. "Perhaps some type of world-important message is waiting to be deciphered," he forecasted sarcastically.

"What on earth are you talking about, Oliver?" asked Mandy Jo.

"The Allcons."

"Why are you always harping on the Allcons?"

"Oh, mom, I'm an Equal Opportunity Religion Stomper, you know that."

Mandy Jo laughed. "You are something else, my son."

"For instance," Oliver continued, "the Cathartics are another bizarre religion. If you're in the Mafia, you can commit murder, go confess your sins, and be forgiven under Catharticism."

"Now Oliver, that's not true," Mandy Jo retorted. "A priest would have to report murder."

"Yeah," Oliver replied with ample sarcasm, "if the priest wasn't pre-occupied ensconcing his gourd in an adolescent wazoo."

"Oh, I knew I couldn't discuss anything with you without you going off the rails," Mandy Jo complained. "Oliver, please don't talk that way."

"Alright, I'll just brush it under the rug like everyone else did…."

"And another thing, mister," Mandy Jo whined, "you're always talking over my head. You know I didn't finish high school. But I admit, you got your smarts from your dad."

"You mean the dad I haven't seen in sixteen years?"

Lisa patted Oliver's knee. "You okay?" she asked. "Now don't get all worked up."

"I know, I go overboard sometimes, but where would we be without me?"

Just then, the movie they were watching cut to a commercial. "We have to put up with these damn commercials all our lives," Oliver fumed. "Capitalist intrusion! And some idiots actually enjoy them!"

"Oliver," said Mandy Jo, now moderately upset. "Do you always have to put things down?"

"Well, I'm not just going to sit here like a mannikin and say nothing. We have to sit at stoplights half the day because of heavy traffic. That's unavoidable. But I'll be damned if I'm going to sit through these annoying commercials. I try to close my eyes and daydream while they're on."

"Maybe you had better take a nerve pill, honey," said Lisa.

"We're just wading through capitalist shit, I tell ya. That's why we're all dumb phonies. Commercials teach one to be phony. What an I'll-Suck-Your-Ass-If-You'll-Suck-Mine racket.

"Oliver!" begged Mandy Jo. "Please stop!"

"OK, then I'll go back to religion. Conservative Spongez never tire of mooching off the world—sucking the blood out of the planet. They've got all the wealth. They *think* they've got all the morals. And now they have the Supreme Court at their grimy little fingertips."

"Oliver, please," implored Mandy Jo. "I'm gonna have to go in the other room."

Lisa made a trip to the kitchen and returned with a Clonepin. "Here, dear, take this," she coaxed.

Even Phoenix went off to hide.

"Some philosopher said," paraphrased Lisa, "that when man begins to question his religion, it will mark the end of civilization."

Oliver swallowed the pill Lisa had given him and continued, "This Conservaprick Gorebingerz romance with Quasar and the Thronez is downright perverse."

Mandy Jo began to whimper.

"These Spongez think they're going to waltz up to heaven right behind the Thronez. Do you know what the Rapture is, Mom?"

"No," Mandy Jo wept, "and I don't want to know."

"It's when all the Spongez weasels go up to heaven after the big Armageddon. But it's all a big bubble, Mom. Waiting to pop. They should call it The Rupture, because the whole damned thing is going to explode. And when the moral bubble ruptures, they will all go sliding down to hell…oh, wait, that's right, because of physics they will all rise to hell. Heat rises, remember."

"If you don't stop," said Mandy Jo between tears, "I'm going to have to call my doctor."

"Mrs. Hicks, don't worry," said Lisa, patting Mandy Jo's knee. "The medicine will take effect in a little while."

"A moral bubble," Oliver added, "is when Gorebingerz want to be so good, they actually digress into an abysmal state of collective mind. When they grow so bad, they will all act stupid in unison. Like they did when they elected Schmidt and then Wackersham, The Peerless Profit. But then the moral bubble will pop."

I don't know what exactly will make it pop, but it is going to happen. Oh, I know, the Guardians of History, those Protectors of Legacy, will record in the annals of our time that The Peerless Profit was merely "abrasive to some parties," and not the bastard that he really is. The Pods of Bubbledumb made sure this creep got in, but the bubble will pop. Maybe I should call it 'Bubbledoom,' 'cause that's what we are with these people in power, DOOMED!"

"What's the Pods of Bubbledumb, Oliver?" asked Mandy Jo, wiping her tears. "I don't even know who you're talkin' about."

"The Pods of Bubbledumb, in general, are the filthy rich, God-fearing Conservapricks. Specifically, they are the ones who live in Blandon-Average...on the *East* side...and other places like Blandon-Average. You know, affluent enclaves and such."

"You mean eclairs?" asked Mandy Jo.

"No!" said Oliver, "*enclaves.* You know, like islands of stupidity."

"But just what the heck *are* these things...these Pods of Bubbledumb?" Mandy half demanded, half implored.

"The Pods grow somewhere out there with the corn. They're like giant cocoons, waiting to hatch. When they do hatch, they become Pod People. They are generally emotionless, snake-eyed soldiers of the field. Their theatre is the behemoth office buildings that have sprung up here and there among the vast corn fields. The Pods operate like nothing bad ever happened in the world—at least not in their little happy town.

"What town?" cried Mandy Jo.

"Any town," snapped Oliver, "where news sources coddle their readers by failing to inform them about the sordid aspects of the planet. They insulate their readers inside a life-is-all-great bubble. Specifically, Blandon-Average, on the east side of town is where the Pods flourish. It's a perfect environment for Pod hatchlings to prosper. They are stiff, stoical plant beings, not necessarily human. They walk in dazed indifference to their surroundings…to the Conservaprick Sins. They masquerade as conservative humans, but they are more like insensitive plants.

"Oh my God!" cried Mandy Jo. "You don't really believe this, do you, Oliver?"

"Mom," explained the neo-hippie, "every time I exaggerate about something, you take me literally. It's called hyperbole, mother. There are not literally pods. They are people who behave as if they were grown in pods. You know, like plants instead of humans."

"Oh dear, you know I'm not good with big words, son."

Oliver began to speak more softly as the medication started to take effect. Another commercial appeared on the screen (they had missed the entire movie segment between commercials). Oliver explained calmly, "In the past, commercials were just plain silly. People used to say, 'They insult my intelligence.' Now they are clever and charming. In fact, commercials today compete to be the most charming. Sometimes they fail; sometimes they resonate with the modern viewer. Soon, the talented writers will leave movies to write commercials. I think they already have. Just look at this terrible movie we're watching. It was made by an idiot."

"I don't even know what it's about," complained Mandy Jo, "because you won't let me watch it!"

Oliver, now growing drowsier, continued his tirade against humanity. "The goal of capitalism is to keep people buying; discard the old and buy the new, no matter how quickly we fill the landfills with American trash. 'Who cares that we use up the earth faster than we can replenish it. Just keep buying and keep quiet. We'll provide high-tech gadgets, spicy food, and slick commercials to keep you all satisfied.' Keep the capitalist machine running until we destroy ourselves."

With that, Oliver yawned loudly and closed his eyes. Mandy Jo and Lisa watched the rest of the movie.

GIVING TUG A JUMP

As Tug drove down I-57, he began to reflect on past events. He thought about growing up in Wheeling, Illinois, wandering along Dundee and Wolf Roads, playing cowboys and Indians in the tall grass, and throwing rocks at birds. He delved deeper into his memories, and both the bad and the good surfaced.

"I told you, you little sonofabitch, not to eat any of those goddamn doughnuts," roared Mr. McRae, his old man. The miserable old bastard smacked him in the face hard. "What'll it take to make you listen, you ugly fatass!"

Tug shook with fear.

"Do I have to do surgery on your stupid ears?" Mr. McRae pulled a pair of jumper cables from the large tool chest in the garage. He then pulled down on Tug's left ear with his calloused fingers, opened the grip with his mighty hand and clipped it onto the fatty part of the lower ear. Tug screamed in utter agony.

"Don't you fucking pull that off! I'll kill you if you do!"

Mr. McRae used the other end of the jumper cable to clip Tug's right ear.

"Ooooowwwww! Daddy, please take it off! Dad-dad-dy please!"

"You'll have to wear those for 60 seconds, son. You did a bad thing, and punishment is final!"

•••

Four days after that horrifying incident, Tug yet smarting in both ears, his old man let him go out to play. Momentarily, Tug's pain sank to the second level of his thoughts.

The white opossum ran in circles inside the large plastic barrel. Tug carelessly duct-taped a butcher knife to the end of an old broom handle and began stabbing the hissing creature. For every miss, there was a hit, and soon the creature, still running around the bottom of the barrel, had red blotches scattered on its white fur. With each downstroke of the broomstick, the opossum grew slower until it finally rolled onto its side and began convulsing. Even that did not last long, as the creature took its last tortured breath.

Tug shuddered with excitement as he came back to the present. B-b-b-b-b-b-brum! The sound of his truck running over the rumble strips on the edge of the pavement startled the big driver, and he weaved momentarily before finding his way back to the outside lane. Soon he exited the expressway and drove to an old motel—The Sundown Motel—near Bradley, Illinois. It did not take him long to meet a haggardly middle-aged woman with no teeth, scraggly hair, and a large scar on her cheek. She was obviously hopped up on meth. Tug talked her into the passenger seat rather quickly. Just three minutes later, he was strangling her in the back of his modern cab.

"I want to fly like a gypsy!" dizzily claimed the poor, wretched soul.

"I fucking hate gypsies!" roared Tug. "Besides, gypsies don't fly, bitch!"

When his business was done, he put on his jump suit and headed down Illinois Route 17 with his latest victim laid out on his bed in back. He then jumped on I-55, cruised down to Funk's Grove and dumped the body among the maple trees on Old Route 66. Two eyeballs on sticks stared up at the three-quarters moon, while the crickets sang an early evening song in the faint, warm breeze of an otherwise still August night.

THE RUPTURE

"Oliver," said Mandy Jo, "There's chicken salad in the fridge if you and Lisa get hungry."

"Ok, mom."

"Did I tell you that me 'n' Tug are goin' on a road trip this Friday?"

"A road trip? You sure you feel comfortable doing that, mom?"

"We'll be fine, hon'. It's just a day trip. Tug is in Missouri now. He's picking me up on Thursday afternoon when he'll be heading back to the Chicago area. I'll be staying at the Hamlin

Inn in Joliet while Tug sleeps at home. He'll pick up a new load on Friday morning, and then we're leaving for East St. Louis. We'll be back on Friday evening."

"I don't know, Mom. Phoenix doesn't trust that guy, and I'm not sure I do either."

"It'll be fine, Oliver."

"So," said Oliver, "you'll leave me the car keys?"

"Yes. So long as you don't smoke those twigs while driving."

"No twigs, mom," Oliver reluctantly agreed. "Oh, here's Lisa now." Oliver opened the door for her and they embraced.

"Hi, Oliver!" said Lisa.

"How was your meeting?" asked Oliver.

"It went well. We decided on a press release…if we don't get censored."

"What kind of a meeting did you have, Lisa?" asked Mandy Jo.

"With the Thronez Push for Reason, Mrs. Hicks."

"They officially declared Quasar an Apartheid State, mom," said Oliver.

"An Apart Hide—what's that?"

"It's a system of racial segregation, Mrs. Hicks," replied Lisa.

"Well, kids," noted Mandy, "you know what they say, that Thronez are the 'Select' people. So, you'd better let Quasar manage itself."

"Mom," said Oliver with frustration, "that's exactly the kind of nonsense we're up against."

"Oliver, are you calling me a fool?"

"No, Mom, I'm not. It's just a foolish statement." Oliver paused and thought for a moment. "I'm sorry, Mom. But if someone tells you that Thronez are 'The Select People,' laugh in their face. And if someone tells you that Thronez are bad, scold them mercilessly. There are no 'bad' people; there are no 'select' people. The latter is Thronez-Gorebingerz nonsense. The former is racism. We are all equal. It takes an ignorant Gorebingerz to say that Thronez are the Select people. Believing that nonsense is just ignorant and unthinking. The Borah and the Babble are both full of rubbish—folk tales that evolved into nonsense. And neither one should give Quasar the right to build houses on occupied land, segregate the Pulsarian people, and oppress them."

The conservative right in this country amounts to a mass of lunatics, buying into this giant mound of horse manure. They have reached too far into the realm of no return. They're probably hopeless, but I'll keep fighting them, anyway."

Lisa thought for a moment, then added, "And so-called President Wackersham isn't fixing the situation, Mrs. Hicks. Not by pandering to the Thronez and not by suggesting that the American Embassy should be moved to Thronezville. What's even stranger is that many of the groups supporting Wackersham are completely racist—against Thronez, against blacks, or anyone who doesn't fit into their narrow view of how someone should be."

"Oh, my goodness," cried Mandy Jo, "please don't get Oliver started on our fine President, dear."

"You mean our Piece-of-Shit President," Oliver corrected his mother.

"Please don't," Mandy Jo implored.

Oliver said, "Wackersham and the Spongez are both aggravating the situation!"

"There he goes...."

"When the so-called Rapture comes," noted Oliver, "those Spongez will all be jacking each other off as they ascend to what they *think* is going to be 'heaven.'"

"Oh, my God, Oliver, stop!" cried Mandy Jo.

"I'll tell you about The Rapture, mom," lectured Oliver. "But I call the whole Wackersham-Spongez thing *The Rupture*. These Spongez will keep draining everything on earth, just as they've been doing. Because they have money, they believe they are closer to their ridiculous God than the less fortunate. All the while, they are eagerly anticipating The Rapture! But it will be The Rupture. They think they are so special that their lives must be extended into eternity just for believing in nonsense! They will consume every resource the earth has to offer in their twisted plan to float up into a utopian heaven."

"Oh, stop him, Lisa!" whined Mandy Jo. "He's making me nervous!"

"Oliver," cautioned Lisa, "you had better take it easy."

"But let me tell you, they will ascend into hell! That's right, because heat *rises*. That's physics, something the fairy tale Babble would never teach you. And when they rise into hell, those filthy Gorebingerz—I'm talking about the ones who believe in that

Spongez-Wackersham bullshit, not the regular Gorebingerz—will find that the moral bubble will have bursted!"

"Oliver, it's OK," Lisa comforted her fiancé. "Settle down, dear."

"Oh God!" wailed Mandy Jo. "Please get it all out before Tug stops by. Please, Oliver, before he gets here."

"Just one more thing," said Oliver, calmer now. "Their buddy, Horace Broadmouth, conservative commentator, is further exasperating the whole issue. He has continually divided us Americans and he deserves to drink toilet water."

"Horace who?" inquired Mandy Jo.

"He's a conservative radio talk-show hate peddler," explained Lisa calmly, "upon whom the President has so ridiculously bestowed the Medal of Freedom."

HAIL THE MIGHTY CHIEF, MAY HE WALK IN THE LORD'S FOOTSTEPS

"Buttercup!" cried Melvin to his makeup-caked wife, "it is wonderful!"

"What is that, hon'?" asked Melanie.

"Do you remember when Schmidt officially recognized Thronezville as the Capital of Quasar?"

"Why, yes dear, I do."

"Well, President Wackersham has just recognized Quasar as the official Thronez State!"

"Oh, why that *is* wonderful!"

"How blessed are we dispensationalists," praised Melvin, "that the Godly Ghant has acted in our favor!" Melvin shed a tear, and Melanie followed.

"I am overwhelmed with joy, dear Melvin!"

"End Times are near, my glorious little Buttercup. Praise Lord Gore!"

"Yes, Melvin, the Lord works in mysterious ways. Just when those Librhoids were preparing their little impeachment game, Ghant rises to the top and makes them all quiver in their loafers!"

"Indeed, my Angel. The Lord has chosen Ghant to be the vessel of blessing! May God's eternal light continue to shine upon us! Glory to our restless hearts!" Melvin wiped away a tear with a fresh tissue. "This calls for a splendid celebration!"

"What shall we do to celebrate, dear?" asked a joyful Melanie.

"Well, I thought we would go to that new restaurant on Soldier's Parkway and give a toast to the Almighty. Then, perhaps we could go to the driving range and practice a bit."

Maybe come home and listen to *Prayers, Hymns and Psalms* by the Baskerville Holy Orchestra with The Choir of the New Century Healers."

"That would be glorious, Melvin. Dear, you are the gospel of my soul."

"And you, Melanie, are the tulip of my dreams."

"Melvin, life is absolutely marvelous. But I long for you in the afterlife."

"And likewise, Buttercup. It is all great. The only thing we could possibly ask for now is a war with Iran."

HIS MAJESTY'S BRIBE

"Elma," explained Maria over the phone, "Back in 2018, Schmidt was offering military assistance to a foreign leader in exchange for dirt on his opponent, Joe Boredom. That amounts to a bribe in my eyes. But Wackersham has actually paid for dirt on his opponent! Just think, the President of the United States bribing a foreign leader. Am I really witnessing this stuff? God, pinch me."

"Well, Maria," responded Elma, "you know I don't like talking badly about people. But America is not in a good place right now."

"I'm not so nice, Elma. I hope they impeach the bastard for a third time. Impeach him and convict him. I mean, this has to stop."

"The Conservaprick's just don't seem to care, Maria."

"They are oblivious to that man's manipulation, his duplicity, his childish hysterics. It's like a rotten apple that nobody wants to pick up, much less take a bite of." Maria's voice trembled at this point in the conversation.

"Or nobody even wants to acknowledge," said Elma.

"Oh, I'm telling you," griped Maria. Then, after a short pause, she said, "How is Tyrel?"

"Oh, he's doing well. All he wants to do is play with the band. His dad wanted to take him to the zoo last week, but he said, 'No, I'll miss band practice.'"

"That little stinker," laughed Maria. "He just wants to play his music, huh, and to heck with everything else!"

"Uh-huh," agreed Elma. "I told him 'You're going to hurt your dad's feelings. He only gets to see you once a week,' but he said, 'No. I'll explain to him.'"

"Well, maybe Tyrel will make it big and buy you a new house or something," said Maria. They both laughed. "Well, tell him that Maria wishes him luck."

"I sure will. You know, so far he's keeping up his grades. But I told him, 'The minute those grades start to slip, that's the end of the band business, Mister.'"

A LOOK TOWARD CANADA

Oliver and his friend Jamelle walked home from class on a chilly September afternoon. Old Mr. Avondale could hear the two as he hauled out the trash.

"These conservative Gorebingerz kook balls are dangerous," preached Oliver. He took a big drag of a joint and passed it to his curious friend, Jamelle.

"How so," wondered Jamelle.

"They are wealthy and they think that their God has bestowed them with such wealth. With that, they expect to gain power, and they are."

"What will that mean to us?" asked Jamelle.

"It means," said a surprised Oliver, with a tight, throaty grunt while letting out his held breath, "at worst, that your irrepressible appetite for sex will have to be curbed. That you shall only have sex to procreate and NOT for enjoyment. It means that girls will be forced to wear dresses all the way down to their ankles. It means you'll have to attend church and pray four or five times a day. It means you'll be compelled to burn all your favorite rock and rap albums." Oliver took another drag. In a muffled voice, he said, "It also means…"

He exhaled a thick puff of smoke and continued, "That colorful album featuring Jimi Hendrix's fingers gliding across the fretboard like they were on skates will crackle in the flames of the bonfire built by the self-righteous do-gooders. That record with Thom Yorke's voice soaring into the ethereal stratosphere will sizzle like burning hair in a bonfire…like cotton candy melts in saliva."

"Naw!" protested Jamelle. "Hell no, man! There are too many of us who will resist!" He handed Oliver the joint. "Ain't there?"

"Not when the Gorebingerz dullards seize control of the military and police." Oliver took one last toke of the roach and threw it away in frustration.

"Ah, fuck! That burns!"

"See," said Jamelle, "you're already going up in flames!"

"But I'm dead serious, Jamelle. With money they can buy power."

"Dude," Jamelle retorted, "I'm moving to Canada when that shit happens."

"You want to step inside for a minute?" asked Oliver, as they walked up to his and Mandy Jo's tiny, Section 8 bungalow on Canopy Street.

"Just for a minute, dude. I'm starving and my mom cooks meatloaf on Tuesdays. That's my favorite."

The two young men went inside and Oliver flicked on the television. They heard the latest news about the serial killings. "As society grows more complex," Oliver noted, "murders multiply. We live in a mega-schizo society."

"You mean like '21st Century Schizoid Man?'"

"Exactly, Jamelle. That song was an incredibly prophetic piece of music."

"Sure thing," agreed Jamelle.

"OK, back to the religious nuts. Today, there are numerous militant groups led by ignorant hillbillies who dictate their manifestos. While these groups are currently disorganized and disconnected, there are signs that they might start to unite. That's concerning enough, but the real threat to America comes from the Gorebingerz fundamentalists, including the wealthy conservative Spongez, Allcons, and Cathartics. These people seek not just financial dominance but complete social control. I'm talking about the suit-and-tie conservative Gorebingerz. Now they have the dirt-poor hillbilly Gorebingerz on their side, especially since the Librhoid Party effectively lost them when Will and Mallory Winston sold out to the corporations."

"Yeah," added Jamelle, "I read that these fringe groups are indeed starting to unite online. That would be a mess if they manage to form a coalition with the affluent Gorebingerz."

"On top of that," you know, "the Gorebingerz and the Thronez have kind of teamed up against the Muzzles."

"Well," said Jamelle, "I wouldn't go that far."

"Well," reasoned Oliver, "This Gorebingerz alliance with Quasar and Thronezville is downright perverse. And Wackersham, the Peerless Profit, will do whatever it takes to please both the Gorebingerz and the Thronez to secure their votes."

"How so?"

"His divisive rhetoric and actions will spell doom for us all. Like when his ally, Schmidt, allowed Thronezville to host the U.S. Embassy. This kind of action will only escalate the conflict between Muzzles nations and Thronez-Gorebingerz nations."

"But how are they gonna get away with it? I mean, the Thronez and Gorebingerz."

"Get away with what?" asked Oliver.

"Well," said Jamelle, "bullying the Muzzles?"

"Oh, dude," said Oliver, "The government of Quasar gets away with anything they want. It's because of The Annihilation. The Gorebingerz are all too familiar with the murder and torture from The Annihilation during World Gore II. It's the greatest tragedy modern man has ever faced. There's no denying that. But because of that, the Gorebingerz are reluctant to criticize Quasar's oppression of Pulsarians…or anything else for that matter."

"So, is it prejudice against Thronez to speak out about it?"

"No, no dude. I'm not prejudiced against anyone or anything. Questioning Quasar isn't being anti-Thronez. You've misunderstood what I'm saying. My girlfriend is a Thronez. How could I be prejudiced? What I'm saying isn't aimed at the Thronez or their religion. It's the Quasar government I'm criticizing. That government is full of far-right extremists. Like Wackersham, the totalitarian jackass. (Jamelle burst into laughter at the term "totalitarian jackass.") Come on dude, I'm not saying anything bad about the people of Quasar. Just the government."

And the ignorant Anglo-Saxons who worship Quasar and choose to look the other way when they perform misdeeds. Besides, dude, the government of Quasar wants you to question any criticism against the Thronez State. They label any criticism as anti-Thronez."

"OK, dude," said Jamelle, "I wasn't insinuating in any way that you are prejudice. I know you're not the bigoted type. You're my bro'."

"That's right, Jamelle. Through thick and thin."

"OK, dude, gotta run. I've got a lot to digest, including some food. I'll talk to you tomorrow."

"Have a good one."

The front door slammed shut, and Oliver stared for a while at the tapestry covering the living room recliner. When he got stoned, he tended to lose himself in the intricate design.

THE MAGIC TAPESTRY

Oliver's mind melted into the multi-colored tapestry like spilled syrup soaks into a thin gown. He lost himself in the birds and flowers of the design. He wandered down a path at the heart of the decorative fabric, which led him to a sunny valley where a symphony of cumulus clouds drifted. These fluffy clouds, resembling cotton candy, hovered in the sky, briefly obscuring the sun, which delighted in casting its rays upon the charming village below.

Soon, the path transformed into a road that split into two distinct lanes. One lane was marked with a sign that read "Enchanted Lane," while the other bore a sign that said "Doomed Lane." Oliver chose the Enchanted Lane. A cluster of quaint cottages perched on a nearby hill, as radiant red, orange, and purple mountains serenaded the valley with their otherworldly melodies.

Oliver continued down the road that led him past the cottages and out of the village. Before long, he arrived at a new town, a peculiar place that felt like it belonged to another era. At the town's entrance, he noticed a banner hanging from a rope strung above the road. The banner read "Welcome Home Troops." He then realized that the town was celebrating a World Gore II victory. Another sign posted nearby read "Pleasant Ridge Population 5,283."

Oliver made his way into a filling station that sold Red Mountain gasoline. The station, resembling a house with its gleaming white shingles and an arched canopy over the pumps, offered various grades of fuel from tall, slender pumps. A bell hose on the newly paved driveway chimed to alert the attendants of a vehicle arriving for service. Two attendants, clad in crisp white uniforms and billed caps, quickly emerged. One attended to the front windshield, while the other lifted the hood to check the oil. Adjacent to the old filling station was a tourist court and some rustic cabins, awaiting tired travelers.

The office was a white cottage, the U-shaped tourist court was built with Ozark rocks in many brown and white shades, and the cabins were covered in painted brown shingles. Pop sold for a nickel a bottle from hulking refrigerator-like machines with long, vertical, oval windows that showed tiny logos on the tops of caps on the bottles, which were set sideways on a rack. Above a money slot, a sign read, "5 cents a pop!" Several machines lined up on a concrete platform adjacent to the office. Across from the first row of the motor court, nestled among the charming cabins, was a modest restaurant named the Red Mountain Inn.

A brightly lit neon sign on a V-shaped pole caught Oliver's eye; it reminded him of the old Ray's Roundup Restaurant sign, where he would later have his first date with Lisa.

Everyone Oliver met was a wellspring of joy. The air was filled with a perfect cheerfulness that seemed to bounce off every surface, infusing every home and business in the neat, magical town. Happy thoughts sprang up like lively dandelions on a sandlot.

As night descended on the peaceful town, fireflies, moons, and stars filled the sky, creating a dazzling display of brilliant colors and light trails for any onlooker to admire.

One gigantic moon hung over the golden-splashed peaks of the mountains on the East side of the public square. Fluorescent fishes swam through the air while glowing owl eyes peered through the magic trees.

"Oliver!" said Mandy Jo in a raised voice. "Wake up, man! You're scarin' me!"

Oliver fell out of his trance somewhat startled.

"You were staring at my recliner again like you were asleep with your eyes open. You OK? Is it the tapestry that makes you so spellbound?"

ALL BY HIMSELF

"Wackersham's gonna do it," boasted Tug to Mandy Jo. "He's gonna give us back our country."

"Give 'us' back our country?" challenged Oliver.

"Us. The white people. He's gonna deliver this country back to the hard-working people who built it."

"Just so you know, Tug," Oliver snapped with sarcasm, "when you say 'the people who built it,' that includes everyone. I mean, what about the Black individuals who labored in the fields picking cotton and tobacco so your ancestors could live in those mansions—err, plantations, I should say?"

"There ain't no Black folks who did anything for me," Tug shot back defiantly.

"What about the Black workers who moved north to build your cars?" Oliver continued. "And what about the Chinese laborers who constructed the railroads out West?"

Tug looked bewildered, clearly irritated by the pointed remarks. "I don't know what you're talking about," he grumbled, his patience waning with the perceptive hippie.

"You really don't, do you?"

"Are you ready to go, Mandy Jo. Your son's disrespectin' me."

"I'm not disrespecting you," said Oliver, "I'm just telling you facts."

"I don't need no damn facts. Matter a fact, I don' need nothin' from nobody, no blacks, no Chinamen, no Martians, no nothin'. Everything I got, I worked for. You understand? I'm a self-made man."

"Oliver," said Mandy Jo, "don't forget to feed Phoenix. We'll see you later."

As soon as they left, out came old Phoenix from the closet in which he was hiding. His fur was a bit disheveled, as he rubbed against Oliver. "I know, old fellow. He's like a venereal wart. You just can't get rid of him."

ERUPTION!

Melanie's body rushed with excitement, yet she felt trepidation concerning her future with Melvin, which exhausted much of her energy. A nervous uneasiness rolled through her veins. To relieve her aching mind, she began to dream of having sex with her young secretary, Emily Carter, a voluptuous maiden with olive skin, bulging breasts and rich, black hair. Melanie could hold back no longer. She pulled down her slacks, inserted her hand inside her underwear, and began to masturbate noisily. "Oh my God," she purred as her fingers moved up and down, round and round. She imagined rubbing vaginas with sweet Emily and quickly arrived at mad orgasm, first moaning, then shouting in unrestrained ecstasy. Her chest heaved as she released one final, ecstatic cry: "Iyoooooooooo Baby!" She sank back onto her satin sheets, letting out a contented sigh. The tension that had gripped her seemed to evaporate, and her earlier worries now felt trivial. Just then, a car door slammed outside. "It must be Melvin!" she realized immediately. Melanie quickly wiped herself with a tissue, adjusted her slacks, and checked her hair in the mirror. With a practiced smile, she headed to the front door to greet Melvin. As she turned the lock, she murmured, "Oh Lord, forgive me, for I am a sinner."

SNOBBY BOBBY

Elma stepped into the back room to watch Mad Spectrum practice for a moment. They were such a lively five-piece band, whose music she did not understand. Elma listened to the lively rhythm Tyrel provided, impressed by how his drumming captured the essence of the jazz-fusion percussionists he admired. She closed the door gently and walked back to the living room. When the band took a break, she picked up the phone and dialed Maria's number.

"Hello," said the hard-working Latina.

"Hello, Maria? What's up sweetie?"

"Oh, not much. Just got off work. Say, this is your day off, isn't it?"

"Yes," replied Elma, "but the band is practicing, so I'm kind of in jail, if you know what I mean." Both women giggled.

"Oh, poor thing," said Maria. "Do you know, I had the rudest customer today."

"Oh, how so?"

Elma listened as Maria recounted the incident.

"Well, apparently, the guy didn't get service as quickly as he expected it. So, he came up to the front of the restaurant and said in a most snotty tone, 'That goddamn waitress walked right by and looked at me straight in the eye, then just kept walking. I've been waiting for ten minutes, and I want some fucking service!' I said, 'What waitress, Bobby?'—he had a nametag on his shirt—and he said, 'The ditzy blonde over there by the fountain,' pointing like a jackass. I said, 'That's not the waitress assigned to your section, and I don't appreciate you talking like that about my workers. Just a minute and I'll find out why your waitress has not yet served you.'"

"The minute they start cursing," Elma said, "I would just turn around and walk away."

"I know," said Maria, "I should have done that, but I didn't on account that I might get fired."

Anyway, the guy walked out...didn't even give me a chance to investigate the reason for slow service. You know, the customer is God in this business."

"Oh my," said Elma, "there are some rather snobby people in Blandon-Average."

"You bet there are! And now, with their nutcase buddy in the White House, they've grown yet more bold, arrogant and snotty…especially those from the East Side."

"I'm just glad I live on the west side," said Elma.

LISA GROWS ILL

"What are you up to?" asked Lisa upon entering the living room of the simple house on Canopy Street.

"I just got done with my homework," answered Oliver. "Getting ready to watch a flick."

"What did you have in mind?"

"Some good old-fashioned American violence, I guess."

"Oliver, no!" cried Mandy Jo. "Ghant is supposed to make a speech. I've had my heart set on watchin' it."

"Oh shit!" griped Oliver. "C'mon, I just saw that arrogant bastard on the news. I can't bear to wa--."

"Oliver, this is my only enjoyment, since Tug is out of town."

"Mom, the only reason we are stuck with that guy is because they didn't prosecute Schmidt for his crimes. They let him do whatever he wanted and did nothing. Now America is paying for it with Wackersham!"

"Oh, Oliver," griped Mandy Jo, "you like who you want, and I'll like who I want."

Oliver grabbed a magazine from the rack next to the couch. "Check this out—what writer Joel Messina of the Public Underground says about your nutball hero: 'Schmidt, himself, made for an uncouth scalawag, but even he stood on a higher rung on the ladder of human worth than the sub-dregs stinkpot known as Wackersham.'"

"Oliver, I…I suddenly feel sick," said Lisa in a strained voice.

"Am I making you nervous?" said Oliver. "Sorry. I'll quit."

"No, that's not it," replied Lisa. "I just feel rundown and a bit nauseous."

Can I use your restroom?"

"Go right ahead, dear," said Mandy Jo. "Are you gonna be OK?"

"I don't know…I'm so dizzy, I could faint."

"Oh dear, do you want me to call an ambulance?" asked Mandy Jo.

"No, I think I'll be alright," answered a woozy Lisa.

Lisa made her way to the restroom, but did not come out. After a few minutes Oliver knocked on the door but got no answer. He ran to the kitchen and got a butter knife, which he slid between the jamb and the door lock. Soon, he opened the door and saw Lisa passed out on the floor. "Call 911, mom! She's fainted." Blood trickled down her face from where she had probably hit her head on the sink or bathtub.

After some harrowing moments, the ambulance arrived. Soon, Lisa was outstretched on a gurney. The medical team had her out the door in a thin moment. Oliver and Mandy Jo followed the ambulance to Springfield Memorial Hospital. The EMT's rushed her to the emergency room, and came out looking puzzled.

"Sir," asked a female EMT, "were you with her all day?"

"No," cried a distressed Oliver, "she was at the Red Cross building doing some volunteer work. What do you think is wrong with her?"

"We're not sure," answered the male technician.

"It could be a case of food poisoning," said the female technician. "But she's in good hands, sir."

"Is she still talking?" asked Oliver.

"She was talking…just a bit. She's kind of in and out right now. But her vitals are fair."

The minutes crept by and Oliver and Mandy Jo heard nothing. Finally, the hospital staff asked the two to go into a private room. About five minutes later a Doctor Chavez entered the room.

"Lisa is in critical condition," said the doctor. "We think it is pancreatitis, but we're still running some tests. Do you know where her parents might be? Hospital staff says they cannot reach them." "They're in Cancun, Mexico on vacation," Oliver replied. Then, in a paranoid manner, he asked, "Do you think she could have been poisoned? She is an outspoken critic of Quasar. Perhaps they poisoned her?"

"No, no," the doctor quickly dismissed the idea. "Like I said, we are still conducting tests, but we have pretty much ruled out any kind of poison."

A petrified but embarrassed Oliver waited another hour, then asked the front desk for a status. The lady at the desk told Oliver that Lisa was in a "very grave condition." Meanwhile, a nurse had retrieved from Lisa's purse a phone number for the hotel where her parents were staying. The nurse informed Oliver that her parents had been contacted and were taking the first flight home.

After more waiting, Oliver asked if he could see Lisa. The staff informed him that he could not and that they could no longer give out information regarding Lisa's condition. Oliver then drove Mandy Jo back home, as she had to go to work at her custodial position at the local grade school.

He then returned to the hospital to wait on Lisa's parents. He fell asleep on a couch in the waiting room.

EARTHLY DEMISE OF A SPIRITED ALTRUIST

Finally, Lisa's parents arrived. It was 3 o'clock in the morning. They woke up Oliver, who was sleeping on a couch in the waiting area. The parents liked Oliver, but they wanted their daughter, in the end, to marry a Thronez. But in the tragic situation they were facing, they treated Oliver like a son.

"Lisa had been feeling bad lately," said Mrs. Westman, "but I didn't realize it was this serious. I should have made her go to the doctor early on."

"Now don't go blaming yourself, dear," said Mr. Westman.

Just then, Lisa's parents were called to a private room. They gave Oliver permission to accompany them.

"You are Lisa's mother and father?" asked Dr. Kowalski.

"Yes," cried Lisa's mother, "my God, what happened."

"The patient has been diagnosed with severe acute pancreatitis. This is a very serious and aggressive case, I'm afraid. We will continue to monitor Lisa constantly and treat her with utmost care."

Lisa's mother sobbed, and her husband embraced her. Oliver sagged in his seat.

"I don't understand it," Oliver asserted as he sat up straight. "She was acting fine when she came over this afternoon. And all of a sudden...."

"Can we see her?" asked Mrs. Westman.

"We can allow just one parent to see her, but only for a minute," said Dr. Kowalski.

When Lisa's mom came back to the waiting room, she was highly distressed. "Oh, it's terrible," she cried. "She's full of tubes and...."

It was only forty minutes later that both Dr. Chavez and Dr. Kowalski came out and asked everybody back into the private room.

"I'm afraid Lisa has passed," said Dr. Kowalski.

"Oh, no, nooooooo!" Mrs. Westman cried.

"I am very sorry," said Dr. Kowalski.

Lisa's mother now burst into a sobbing fit. Her father slumped his head and hugged Mrs. Westman.

And in that instant Oliver lost control of himself. He slid off his chair and onto the floor where he wept like a cheated child. He could not bear the suddenness of this brutal episode. He knew his life would never be the same again.

•••

The night stretched long and cold, its grip tightening like the sinister Illinois Eye Digger's hold on his victims. In Springfield, Illinois, the dawn was dreary, heavy with the chill of a drizzle that had begun to fall. Dark clouds shrouded the moon, casting an eerie pall over the town. Oliver felt as though Lisa's spirit was drifting through the bleak atmosphere, merging with the somber surroundings.

His drive home was a blur, a succession of empty moments he couldn't recall. When he finally reached his house and collapsed onto the couch, the morning light was a mere struggle against the encroaching gloom. Exhausted from his grief, Oliver wept himself into a troubled sleep, the sun's hesitant rays barely piercing the heavy clouds outside.

WORN AND WILTED

The next few days were draped in a deluge of depression. To Oliver, it was like nothing wanted to move. In the aftermath of Lisa's death, Oliver felt as if the world had come to a standstill, overwhelmed by waves of grief that inundated his mind. His memories of the funeral services were fragmented, clouded by a succession of blackouts that left him adrift in a storm of sorrow. The weight of Mrs. Westman's tears and the somber duties as a pallbearer were but distant echoes amidst the emotional maelstrom.

As he slowly began to surface from the depths of his despair, Lisa's memory continued to haunt him, consuming his thoughts. Seeking solace, Oliver turned to REM, Lisa's favorite rock band, hoping to connect with her spirit through their music. The songs wrapped around him, their melancholic melodies and poignant lyrics providing a semblance of comfort. In the darkened space, he reached out, yearning to touch her soul, though he often questioned if it was merely an emotionally charged illusion.

With the customary services behind him, Oliver retreated into a cocoon of sleep, finding temporary escape from his pain. For the next three days, he remained largely in a state of exhaustion, his days blending together in a haze of rest and contemplation.

Finally, he knew that he had to go back to work and school, so he begrudgingly labored to shower, dress, and check back into the world he had left behind over a week before.

•••

The first day back at work proved highly difficult for the depressed young man, but he struggled forward and endeavored to work to the conclusion of his shift. Oliver, still wallowing in misery and self-pity, came home and greeted Pheonix with loving caresses. He sat down on the couch and stared at the tapestry on the recliner. He thought that a bowl full of Jamaican Yellow-Bud might ease his suffering, so he grabbed his pipe from a dresser drawer in his bedroom and came back in the living room to get high. Mandy Jo was working her custodial job at the school.

Oliver took a half dozen tokes and held them in as long as he could. He certainly copped a buzz, but the misery only seemed to grow stronger. He laid back on the couch and again gazed into the busy tapestry on the recliner.

He found himself one more time following the trail on the cloth and quickly lost himself. This time, when he arrived at the fork in the road, he carefully weighed the options of "Enchanted Lane" and "Doomed Lane" and decided on the latter. Soon, he trudged through knee-deep mud in a dreadful thunder storm. The mud level rose to his waist and then to his chest, and it stank too. Trash began to float by him. Suddenly, coffins began to float by; one almost hit him as it moved past. The world's mess was upon him.

Oliver pushed forward through the rising muck, his clothes and boots weighed down by the thick, stinking mud. The storm raged around him, thunder crashing and lightning illuminating the grim scene. Each step felt like a battle, the mud clinging to him as though trying to pull him under.

Then, rotted corpses began to appear, the heavy rain washing their putrid bodies as they lay atop the thick goop. One armless corpse bumped him, sending chills through his beleaguered body. "Stupid humans," cried the overwhelmed hippie, "and their goddamn coffins…and their goddamn rotting carcasses. Why do they bury and try to preserve their rotting flesh?" Oliver found himself fighting the slow but powerful current of the slime. "Gore fucking Binger, where am I?" he asked himself.

Oliver now breathed heavily while pushing through the thick filth. Garbage from all of the landfills rendered the mud a stew of sorts and crowded out the young rebel. Soon, he had to try and swim, for the putrid stew had swollen to a level that was over his head. He floundered there in the cold stew, half smothered by the fetid gunk, oil slicks, and methane gas fumes. Oliver gasped and choked, as the rain kept pouring and the waste kept rising. The stoned long-hair reached for a bathtub that happened to float by, but his greasy fingers could not hold on. Anything one could imagine drifted through the slimy goo. Here a crappy diaper, there the handlebars from a bicycle. There was an old tube television set, a wagon wheel, a piece of fence, food packaging by the score, a garbage can, a typewriter with broken keys, plastic grocery bags, tin foil slivers, a pair of false teeth, gobs of spoiled food, a smiling skull with decomposing skin still attached around its forehead and cheeks, a dead dog with its rib cage protruding, part of a scoreboard, human and animal entrails, and a ton of deflated balloons that had fallen from the sky after every time a family had to bury a murder victim.

The stew became so thick that Oliver could scarcely move. "Wading through waste is hardly my idea of having a good time after work," said the gunge-laden hippie. "Goddamnit, I'm drowning in shit!"

Oliver, disoriented and embarrassed, quickly sat up on the couch, trying to shake off the remnants of his dream. He looked around, realizing he had been lost in a daydream, and noticed the pungent smell of marijuana lingering in the air.

"Uh, sorry," he mumbled, rubbing his eyes. "I must've dozed off. Just... got a bit caught up in my thoughts."

Mandy Jo gave him a quizzical look, still processing what she had walked in on. "You've been staring at that tapestry again, haven't you? And you know I don't mind if you smoke, but it's not a good idea to mix it with, well, whatever's on your mind."

Oliver sighed, nodding. "Yeah, I guess I got a bit too immersed. Just... had a rough time lately."

Mandy Jo, sensing his distress, softened her tone. "Hey, you want to talk about it? Or maybe just get out for a bit? Sometimes a change of scenery helps."

Oliver appreciated the offer and shook his head. "Maybe later. For now, I think I just need to get a grip on things."

You've been smokin' those twigs again! Open a window. That stuff makes me sick!"

"Theyr'e not twigs, mom—"

"I know, I know! Well, leaves, or whatever they are. It stinks to holy hell!"

WITHERED TITTIES

The REIC Gals met every month. REIC stood for Real Estate Investment Club, which mainly consisted of East Side women from Blandon-Average. Melanie's enthusiasm was palpable as she guided her guests through her opulent home. The ladies of the club marveled at every detail of her elaborate décor, from the gleaming marble floors to the intricately designed chandeliers.

As she led them through the rooms, Melanie continued her enthusiastic commentary. "And here we have my handcrafted Italian leather sofa set. It's not just stylish; it's also incredibly durable and comfortable. You know, this set alone cost more than most people's entire living room!"

The guests exchanged impressed glances, clearly captivated by Melanie's display of wealth and success. The tour continued, with Melanie showcasing her state-of-the-art kitchen appliances, her extensive collection of rare porcelain figurines, and her impressive library, complete with built-in bookshelves and a cozy reading nook.

"Now, let me show you the pièce de résistance," Melanie said with a flourish, leading them to her backyard. "Here is our custom-designed croquet field and the two-hole golf course Melvin had installed last summer. It's perfect for summer afternoons and entertaining guests."

The group admired the manicured lawns and the neatly arranged croquet set. Melanie's pride was evident as she pointed out the details, including the well-maintained greens and the elegant golf course design.

"And, of course," Melanie added with a wink, "in winter, we enjoy Uncle Owen's indoor pool. It's absolutely divine, especially when the weather outside is less than hospitable."

As the tour concluded, Melanie's guests were clearly impressed, their compliments flowing freely. Melanie basked in the attention, her smile broad and satisfied. It was clear that for her, this showcase was not just about her home, but about celebrating her accomplishments and her enviable lifestyle.

Melanie's augmented breasts protruded in firm fashion, as she embellished the description of her many treasures with copious adverbs and adjectives. Her swollen nipples seemed to stand at attention like two sentries guarding a vault full of top-secret, classified documents at a U. S. military base. Old Ms. Fogarty could not remove her eyes from those delightful golden thumbs, as she always harbored a secret crush on the twenty-five-years-younger real estate champion. And the romance blossomed in three directions, since Melvin, who, of course, Melanie adored, had his own fancy with the crusty old widow, Ms. Fogarty. The affluent financial advisor had an inner need to be mothered, and a sexual appetite for the old and sassy. He often masturbated in the shower over Ms. Fogarty's more natural features, and, what he imagined were shriveled, prune-like breasts. Yes, he had actually over-sampled Melanie's oversized, artificial honeydews, and yanked himself into orgasm over the widow's normal-sized orbs.

"And this here is my prized vase…."

HIGH CRIMES AND A GREAT BIG YAWN

With bills gathering on Elma's kitchen table like flies on an animal carcass, the savvy motel-maid considered her options of acquiring more money. She could either borrow from her 401K plan, the funds of which she had accumulated as a computer programmer, or take a second job. She opted for the latter and began working nights as a part-time waitress at Horatio's Restaurante, where her friend, Maria, once worked as a hostess. Meanwhile, she kept sending out resumes for various Information Technology positions. Elma's frustration with the unfolding scandal was palpable. The stark contrast between her own struggles and the corruption at the highest levels of power weighed heavily on her. As she listened to the news, the unfairness of the situation became even more apparent. Her life, dedicated to hard work and honesty, seemed overshadowed by the unchecked greed and corruption of those in power.

The media's dismissal of the scandal and Schmidt's eventual acquittal only deepened her disillusionment. The former President's wealth and influence had shielded him from the consequences of his actions, leaving ordinary people like Elma to grapple with the fallout.

In the years that followed, the public's indifference to the new President's crimes did little to alleviate the sense of betrayal felt by those who had hoped for justice. As Wackersham retired from office, the perception of his legacy remained tainted by the corruption that had marked his tenure.

For Elma, the news was a bitter reminder of the gap between the powerful and the powerless, and the struggle to maintain integrity in a world where justice seemed so often out of reach.

It would be secret-service guarded, pension-bloated retirement in lush surroundings for the marvelous American criminal, and the sane half of the public could do nothing about it.

KABOOM!

One night Oliver walked to the park to meet Jamelle and some other friends. The radical 24-year-old was yet dejected over the loss of Lisa and thought that some fun in the park might soothe his aching mind. The young rebels hung out at a bench near the monkey bars, which kids never used anymore, since they all had smart phones and electronic games to play. The kids told several stories. One story drew a mix of laughter and groans from the gathered crowd. The absurdity of the gods' contest brought a brief, surreal distraction from the concerns of the world outside.

"Man, that's messed up," said one of the guys, shaking his head with a grin. "But you gotta admit, it's kinda funny."

Oliver took a long drag from his joint and exhaled a cloud of smoke. "Yeah, I guess it's just one of those ridiculous things that makes you laugh when you're not taking life too seriously."

The conversation slowly shifted back to the usual topics—music, the latest news, and personal stories—while the night continued with its haze of smoke and camaraderie. Despite the underlying tension and paranoia of the pandemic, moments like these provided a fleeting escape into humor and connection. A couple of joints spiced up the night air, as they went from hand to hand. Even with the Covid paranoia that permeated society, the freaks shared their Jamaican Rainbow Weed.

The common chatter died down for a moment when Oliver suddenly and uncharacteristically told a story: "OK. Three Gods drift into a bar. The bartender asks, 'Which one of you is all-powerful?' The Thronez God looks up and says, 'I must be the all-powerful God, for I can fart the loudest!' Then, the Gorebingerz God says, 'No! I can fart louder than you!' And the Muzzles God says, 'No way. I can fart louder than the both of you!' Now the bartender put on his protective ear mufflers and held his nose. Three tremendous booms in succession shook the bar to its core, each God passing the heaviest wind yet known to mankind. Pictures fell off the walls and drinking glasses tinkled. The bartender rubbed his chin, squatted, and said with his arms outstretched, "Stand aside." He crouched a bit more and cocked his right leg. A fourth and most superior BOOM followed and brought down the walls of the place! All were amazed. Finally, the three Gods got on their knees, bowed, and said in unison: 'Bartender, yours was the mightiest of all farts. Praise thee. Amen!' They all bowed again and kissed the floor. The Thronez God then said, 'There's a new God in town! But how did you do it?' 'That's easy,' said the smug bartender. 'I ate three cans of Pork and Beans, two king-size helpings of Sauerkraut, a helping of broccoli and cabbage, six fried eggs, and three prunes for dinner. Then I did summersaults on the front lawn for half an hour and held it in for as long as I could. That's when you guys came in!' Then the Gorebingerz God declared, 'We have witnessed one of the most thunderous farts that ever shook the heavens! Glory be!'

"Oh, my God!" shrieked Sally Parkinson, before drawing a puff from the shrinking reefer stick. "That's blasphemous! And gross on top of it." The rest of the gang laughed heartily.

JASMINE

"Where will you be in ten years?" asked Tug.

"I dunno," answered Jasmine, a twenty-three-year-old date Tug had lined up.

"I mean, have you ever wondered what is God's plan for you?" Tug's dead eyes slanted a bit.

"Well, I don't really believe in all that religious hocus pocus," said Jasmine. "What happens just happens."

"You mean you don't believe in God?" Tug's teeth began to grind.

"Not really," noted Jasmine. "My higher power is my body. Men are jus' crazy about it, you know."

"So, what about heaven and hell?" asked a stunned Tug.

"What about it?" Jasmine smiled. "I've already walked through hell. I mean, I'm livin', ain't I?"

"So you think this is hell?"

"Well, hell, if there is one, couldn't be any worse than this. Dontcha think?"

Tug boiled like an overdone egg. His lips contorted and his eyes grew yet narrower.

"Well," Tug said in a soft tone, "I'm sorry, but I'm gonna have to choke you out."

"I ain't afraid to die," responded Jasmine with an even softer voice.

The brutal scene unfolded with a chilling sense of finality, each action weighed down by grim determination. Tug's cold efficiency in handling Jasmine's lifeless body betrayed no hint of hesitation or remorse. His words, though laced with a twisted form of respect, highlighted the stark reality of his nature.

As he prepared to dispose of the body, the macabre routine was carried out with a mechanical precision, a stark reminder of the dark and unfeeling world in which Tug operated. The roadside, soon to be the final resting place of Jasmine, remained an indifferent backdrop to the grim act, embodying the harshness of Tug's existence.

SQUEEZING OUT THE LITTLE GUY

"As of tomorrow, dream kitten, I will be an independent financial advisor." Melvin smiled fiendishly. "With most of my clients intact."

"Isn't it wonderful, my dearest Melvin," Melanie said.

"Yes," said Melvin, "and the first thing I'm going to do is draft a letter to drop all of my clients with balances under $500,000. I really need to weed out the poor people, if you know what I mean."

"Yes, dear."

"I mean, why should I have to suffer just because they were low earners or weak savers all their working lives."

Melanie's over-tanned face grew ripe with joy. "You should raise your expense fees too, dear."

"Oh, my little Tulip, I've been working on a plan behind the scenes to do just that. I have settled on a quarter of a percentage point increase in my fees." Melvin took a big bite of his lobster and wiped the creamy garlic butter from his mouth. "Waitress!" he practically shouted across the elegant room. "Could I get a doggie bag and my check, please?"

When the smiling waitress returned with the bag of food, the Two Mels rose from their seats and walked away from the table, leaving no tip. The couple's avarice could not have blazed any brighter were it on a marquee.

Elma Ray's disquieting task of clearing the table was made all the more frustrating by the blatant disregard for proper etiquette displayed by the Two Mels. Their refusal to leave a tip, despite their opulent surroundings and extravagant meal, reflected their greed and lack of consideration.

Elma's commitment to maintaining her own standards of respect and professionalism, even in the face of such behavior, underscored her integrity. While her colleagues might have had their own opinions, Elma chose to rise above the situation, focusing on her duties and keeping her discomfort to herself.

DISGUSTED COHORTS

"You know, Maria," said Elma over the phone. "I don't have to have a Librhoid president. I can go either way. I just want some decency."

"Yes," agreed Maria, "just some good old-school decency would serve us well at this time."

"With that said, Brace yourself for the latest.," cautioned Elma.

"Oh no, now what?"

"Wackersham wants to take away the consumer's ability to sue corporations."

"When did that fathead say that?" asked Maria.

"On the morning show with Lydia Melton."

Maria sighed. "That means a company can outright poison you and not be held accountable? That sick sonofabitch!"

Maria's frustration with the political climate was palpable, her anger simmering over the presence of Wackersham's supporters who seemed oblivious to the damage he was causing. Elma, ever the voice of reason and optimism, tried to offer comfort and reassurance. She believed that despite the chaos and division stirred up by Wackersham and his allies, the resilience and strength of people like Maria would help them deal with the madness.

"And for what it's worth," said Elma, "Wilma Van Horn, the prognosticator, says we'll all be corporate slaves if it's up to Wackersham and the Conservapricks…and that she sees a great cataclysm resulting from Wackersham's divisive rhetoric and draconian views."

"I'm tellin' you," griped Maria. "Those Conservaprick weasels come into the restaurant all the time with their shiny Ghant! pins and their smirky faces, just beaming and basking in the Wackersham afterglow. I just want to grab them by the collars and slap some sense into them, you know. Here, this guy is making a mockery of our democracy and they're sitting there and glowing with their shallow smiles. It throws me into a fit!"

"Take it easy, dear," assured the optimistic Elma. "We'll get through this."

"Conservapricks" noted Maria, "always walk around like they are better than everyone else. Then, they turn around and elect this disgrace of a man, this wretched pile of scum. It makes me sick."

THE SAVIOR

One night Tug and Mandy Jo had just watched a movie when Oliver came home from working a Happy Hamburger afternoon shift.

"I see your boy is goin' down for money laundering, sexual harassment and bribes," noted Oliver, as he tossed his books on the living room table.

"Wha?" replied Tug, "President Wackersham?"

"Well, if you can call him a President," responded Oliver.

"Oh," said Tug, "that's jus' the liberals ganging up on him." He then snickered, "They're trying their damnedest to derail his plans for the rebirth of America."

Tug's mouth was as annoying as flip-flops in an empty gymnasium, thought Oliver. The young student wanted to try and reason with the oafish clod, but he thought, that is like asking a Muzzle to eat swine. It is just not going to happen.

Finally, Oliver blurted, "The world changes; Conservapricks don't."

Just then, Jamelle knocked on the front door. Oliver let him in and led him to his room. "I was just arguing with the world's foremost Wackersham Worshiper," he told Jamelle.

"Yeah," whispered Jamelle, "I know he's your mom's boyfriend and all, and you know I really respect your mom, but I gotta say, that guy seems awfully dumb for being such a smug asshole."

"What can I say," agreed Oliver, "he's a real Cro-Magnon goon."

"You got a joint of that Columbian Dogbud you can sell me?" asked Jamelle.

"Not for sale," replied Oliver. "But I'll give you a joint."

"Cool," said Jamelle. "I got a hot date later on, and I need something to buzz my girl."

Oliver rolled up a healthy-sized number and handed it to his friend.

"All these old mother fucker's just love that lunatic President," griped Oliver. "I'm getting so sick of it."

"Yeah," said Jamelle, "but it isn't just old people. Young people by the millions are lovin' this guy."

"This is what happens," said Oliver, "when you have a modern generation that knows nothing about history. All they know is computers. They wouldn't know a Democracy if it came up and pinched them in the groin."

"Yeah," agreed Jamelle, "they live their lives inside a cellphone."

"They're slaves to the wafer," added Oliver. "The capitalists have arranged for the modern educational emphasis on computers in order to better their business operations. Meanwhile, kids are not learning about the shaping of a democracy. The struggles of laying out and keeping a democracy. And Wackersham sets a bad example, since he knows nothing but making money."

"That scumbag Wackersham has changed everything," noted Jamelle. "It's like we're living in another galaxy."

"To elevate a proven miscreant to a Godly being," said Oliver, "is a most clear demonstration of mental illness."

Oliver lit up an extra joint. Between tokes, he said, "Upon Schmidt's arrest back in 2023, the obedience to his lies and criminality grew like a rising member after a fresh dose of Viagra. And it's the same thing for Wackersham. This goes beyond obsession. This is downright perverted. Just think about it, the population is composed of perverts—40% of us anyway. Perverts who thrive on bad character. Wackersham does something horrendous, and the perverts get more invigorated."

"I just can't understand why they're so enamored with this guy," said Jamelle. "Where's the quality? Where's the character?

Where's the goods? He's like a sinking turd, of no value to anyone. Someone please flush it!"

"Well," explained Oliver, "he's like Gore Binger to them. They pass over all reports of his sinister and criminal acts, as if those reports were tantamount to Gore's persecution before he was burned on the Z platform and cut up into pieces. So you see? Any account of Wackersham's sinister deeds can be construed as just another attempt by the Librhoids at persecuting, what in the Conservaprick's eyes, is the greatest human being who ever set foot on the planet. Suspicions are delusional. Accusations are unwarranted. And investigations into his illegal activity, no matter how egregious his transgressions may seem, are dismissed as 'witch hunts.'"

Oliver and Jamelle finished smoking a big bowl of Columbian Dogbud and sat there saying nothing. Time floated by like a slow-moving, sleepy cloud. Finally Jamelle spoke.

Oliver rolled a joint for Jamelle and passed it to him with a nod. As they settled down, the tension from the earlier argument slowly melted away. They kicked back and let the soothing effects of the Columbian Dogbud take over, their conversation drifting away from politics and into lighter topics.

They reminisced about old times, shared stories about their favorite bands, and discussed their plans for the future. The evening turned into a rare moment of peace and camaraderie, a welcome break from the discord and frustration of the day.

"Cool," said Jamelle. "I got a hot date later on, and I need something to buzz my girl."

Oliver rolled up a healthy-sized number and handed it to his friend.

"All these old mother fucker's just love that lunatic President," griped Oliver. "I'm getting so sick of it."

"Yeah," said Jamelle, "but it isn't just old people. Young people by the millions are lovin' this guy."

"This is what happens," said Oliver, "when you have a modern generation that knows nothing about history. All they know is computers. They wouldn't know a Democracy if it came up and pinched them in the groin."

"Yeah," agreed Jamelle, "they live their lives inside a cellphone."

"They're slaves to the wafer," added Oliver. "The capitalists have arranged for the modern educational emphasis on computers in order to better their business operations. Meanwhile, kids are not learning about the shaping of a democracy. Oliver took another drag from the joint, feeling a bit of relief from the tension in the air. Jamelle leaned back and listened, his expression reflecting both frustration and understanding.

"Exactly," Oliver continued, "it's a bizarre kind of hero worship, twisted beyond recognition. They see any criticism as a personal attack on their deity. Wackersham's like some sort of living myth to them, a symbol of their rebellion against what they see as an unjust system. And they're willing to overlook all his flaws and crimes because they think he's sticking it to the establishment."

Jamelle shook his head. "It's like they're caught in some kind of cult-like trance. The more he screws up, the more they defend him, like they're locked into this cycle of denial and justification."

Oliver nodded, his eyes reflecting the dim light of the room. "It's terrifying to think how easily people can be manipulated. It's as if the more corrupt and vile he becomes, the more it reinforces their misguided loyalty. It's a perverse form of devotion that thrives on chaos and corruption."

They sat in silence for a moment, the smoke curling around them as they pondered the state of their world. The conversation drifted into quieter topics, but the weight of their discussion lingered, coloring their thoughts as they continued to unwind.

Suspicions are delusional. Accusations are unwarranted. And investigations into his illegal activity, no matter how egregious his transgressions may seem, are dismissed as 'witch hunts.'"

Oliver and Jamelle finished smoking a big bowl of Columbian Dogbud and sat there saying nothing. Time floated by like a slow-moving, sleepy cloud. Finally Jamelle spoke.

"You know," he said, "'The Red Telephone' by Arthur Lee and Love is the greatest song of all time."

"Well," countered Oliver, "I wouldn't much argue with that. It's definitely one of the greatest of all time. Except, the song that just sticks in my mind, through all of the joy and agony of my lifetime, is 'Echoes,' by Pink Floyd. It's certainly the deepest song ever written, both literally and figuratively."

"Well, I can't argue with that, either," said a relaxed Jamelle.

"I guess it depends on one's mood," Oliver shrugged. "Different songs are great at different times."

Soon the two friends said "so long" and Oliver sat back on his bed, folded his long arms, and dreamed about plants and animals and the beginning of the universe in the soft, smokey light of his bedroom pot parlor.

A DATE FOR MELANIE

Melvin paced back and forth in his living room, his mind racing as he dialed Tug's number on his cell phone. When Tug answered, Melvin cleared his throat, trying to steady his voice.

"Hi Tug, this is Melvin Goodall. Remember me from the Country Pantry Restaurant in Blandon-Average?"

"Uh, Melvin?"

"Shorter guy, reddish hair. My wife and I had breakfast with you. Melanie, remember?"

"Oh…yeah, yeah. Melanie! I remember. That's a heck of a woman you got there, Melvin"

"How are you?"

"Can't complain. Yerself?"

"Oh, I'm fine. Hey, I was wondering…do you know any—" Melvin cleared his throat—"any prostitutes?"

"Prostitutes, heh. Wha—yer wife ain't doin' it for you anymore?"

"No, no," said Melvin, "nothing like that." Melvin turned red, even though no one was in the room. "You know, "nothing raggy. Maybe someone in the higher echelon of the business?"

"Eshlon??? You talk sorta funny, Melvin."

"Yeah, yeah, someone who is a little better than sleazy. Know what I mean?"

"Well, ah, I know of a couple. What did ya have in mind, a blonde, brunette, someone with big honkers?"

"Yes, well, you see, it's not for me--it's for my wife. And I'm not really sure she has a preference, as long as it is someone decent looking and not a—" Melvin whispered here--"street whore."

"For Melanie? I didn't figure her for goin' both ways. I'll tell you what I'll do. Lemme check into it and I'll get back to you, heh?"

"OK."

"I need your num—oh, I got it right here on my phone. Is this the best number to reach you at?"

"Yes sir," said Melvin, trying to be cool. "And, hey Tug, can we keep this quiet? You know, just the four of us should know, OK?"

"Four of us?"

"Yes, You, me, the prostitute and Melanie."

"OK, yeah, just the four of us. You betcha. See you, Melvin."

"Bye Tug."

Tug sank into his couch, his anger simmering beneath the surface. He took a sip of his lemonade, his thoughts turning darker with each passing moment. The memory of his mother's revolving door of suitors gnawed at him, fueling a twisted sense of revenge.

He let out a harsh laugh. "Serial killer, mass murderer... it's all just a joke now. But who knows? Maybe someday I'll really snap." The idea both horrified and exhilarated him, a dangerous mix of fantasy and frustration.

Tug's gaze fixed on the dent he'd made in the wall, a tangible reminder of his uncontrolled rage. He began to calm down, the excitement fading into a more subdued anger. "For now, I've got to focus on this job. It's just a favor, after all," he muttered, trying to bring himself back to reality.

As he stared at the dent, Tug's thoughts wandered to the potential consequences of his actions. He knew he needed to control his darker impulses, but the thrill of his own dangerous thoughts lingered, a reminder of the thin line he walked between fantasy and reality.

NINE DREAMS

Tug's Dream

Tug approached the hydraulic embalming table with a bold demeanor. He was at last going to have his way with a true cadaver. It was not a fresh corpse, he knew, but he had confidence that he could penetrate it before ejaculating. He carried the limp body—post-rigor mortis--over his shoulder and gently laid it on the table. He pulled a lever to lower the table as far as it would go. He separated the unnamed corpse's legs and unzipped his own britches before trying to mount her. "This is it!" he muttered. "This is finally it!" Suddenly, he felt that irresistible itching in his groin. He raced to position himself for entrance. But it came on in such a rush, he could not hold back. He ejaculated before he could even fully mount the body. "GODDAMNIT!" he yelled.

Tug woke up to find the crotch opening of his pajama bottoms soaked in semen. What kind of strange message is this sending? He asked himself. Something in his life would terminate, he guessed, but what could it be? Frustrated, he bit his index finger with grievous ferocity and reached for some tissues on the bedside table.

Melvin's Dream

Melvin's office was a fortress of exclusivity, designed to shield him from the outside world and its diversities. Inside the heavily fortified space, he maintained a meticulously controlled environment. The twelve-foot thick quadruple-insulated walls kept out any unwanted sounds or influences, ensuring a pristine bubble of isolation.

The elaborate security measures extended beyond the walls. As each visitor entered, Melvin's extensive audio protective gear muffled the external noises, creating an artificial cocoon. He had crafted this environment with precision, reflecting his narrow-minded views and deep-seated prejudices.

When an African-American investor was permitted entry, they were greeted by an imposing thirty-foot table in the center of the room, where a bowl of watermelon candy stood as a token gesture of supposed hospitality. The candy was more than just a sweet treat; it was a calculated, patronizing symbol, embodying the unsettling dynamics of Melvin's approach to his clientele.

The ambiance of the room was a mix of ostentation and segregation, a representation of Melvin's flawed ideology and skewed priorities. The vast space, designed to make a statement, highlighted the disparity and discomfort of those who were forced to navigate this carefully controlled environment.

At this point Melvin shows his client a film of Ghant Wackersham walking upon the waters of The Two Mels' frog pond. No, those waters did not part, for the King walked right upon them.

Melanie's Dream

"Welcome to this wonderful, exclusive East Side dream home, Mr. and Mrs. Saberwinkel. Please remove your shoes for this magnificent tour of the Tabernathy Mansion. Can I get you a bottle of sparkling, filtered Mountain Peak water?" Melanie's voice dripped with insincere enthusiasm as she ushered the potential buyers through the opulent property. Her forced cheerfulness masked her true feelings, as she navigated the delicate dance of high-pressure salesmanship.

She led them with practiced ease, her movements punctuated by a show of grand gestures and glowing descriptions. "Oh, the taste of Blandon-Average is truly remarkable!" she declared with an exaggerated flourish. "This magnificent property is just crying out for an elite, caring couple like yourselves."

With a practiced flick of her hand, she directed them towards the various features of the house. "Would you like to start with the swimming area out back? It's perfect for those serene afternoon swims." Her voice wavered slightly with faux excitement as she continued, "Or perhaps the private bowling alley on the lower level? It boasts two fabulous lanes, one 'His' and one 'Hers'—a true luxury!"

Melanie's eyes sparkled with the pretense of genuine interest, though her mind raced with thoughts of commission and sales goals. "And just look at this four-car garage!" she added, her tone sweet and inviting. "Isn't it just the epitome of convenience and style?"

As she spoke, her practiced smile never faltered, even as she internally judged her clients and the subtle challenges of selling such a grandiose property.

And over here we have...."

Elma's Dream

Elma chased a giant centipede into the darkness of an overcast night. But before she realized the futility of her pursuit the dog-sized thing had overtaken her from behind. A hundred tiny legs skittered up her spine, sending shivers through her entire body. She felt a sudden rush of chills, and then everything blurred into a hazy dreamlike state. Without warning, she found herself trapped in a massive vise, her head tightly bound by a leather strap, as if it were set on a tee. Her tormentor had transformed into a towering, hairy figure wearing a MAWA hat, his face obscured by a ghastly mask. The man, his arms slick with sweat, muscles straining and bulging, raised a 20-pound sledgehammer high above his covered head, pausing to take a deep breath as he held it there for a moment. Elma braced herself for the brain-squishing, life-ending impact. With one tremendous grunt, the man swung it downward upon her skull— "Ah!!!" She woke up to the sound of raindrops gently pitter-pattering against the outside of her bedroom window sill....

Tyrel's Dream

"Ladies and gentlemen, live from Chicago's fabulous Arie Crown Theatre, I bring you Mad Spectrum!" The lights dimmed and the keyboard notes tinkled though the nebulous froth of the prolific fog machine. Then the entire band joined in, and a burst of stars and lunar rainbows flooded the minds of the entranced audience, who were captivated by the cosmic sounds of the fluid new group. Flamboyant chords spiraled up into the timeless sky, and the amazed crowd erupted in boundless cheers. Suddenly, the music broke, leaving them in stunned silence. Then, a feather-light passage caressed their ears and brought angels to their thoughts. The night sank into the ocean of sound and lovingly drowned in tranquil solemnity. Suddenly, a blaze of jazz-rock fusion blistered the air, the audience jumping up and down with controlled passion. Mad Spectrum was a raving success!

Oliver's Dream

Dr. Erlichman bred a spider whose bite generated an ethereal trip. People lined up for miles, eager to have the dream-inducing venom injected into their system by the quivering fangs of one of these psychedelic arachnids. Dr. Erlichman would carefully pick up one of the red-blotched spiders, handling it like a snapping turtle, by its sides, keeping his fingers safely out of reach of its bite. He would then place the spider on a prominent vein on the patient's forearm and gently squeeze it, prompting the creature to release its precious juice. Once the spider had done its job, he would place it in a large canister and reach into a big jar for a fresh one, ready for the next patient. The high was like acid but without the nervous stomach side effects, sort of like heroin, coke and LSD combined. Only Oliver had harbored a deep fear of spiders for most of his life. "Can't you just extract his venom into a vile so I could drink it or something? Please Doc...."

Suddenly, Lisa's face appeared. It was just floating there, but she was saying something. Oliver listened intently. Then he heard it: "Oliver, help me! Oh, please help me!" This startled the tired hippie from his slumber. He wept quietly in the midnight murk.

Mandy Jo's Dream

"Let us have a hand for the greatest President of all time...and perhaps the greatest man of all time... 'The Balanced Sage' himself, Ghant Wackersham!" A tidal wave of cheers reverberated through the ballroom. A fully converted Oliver and an ecstatic Mandy Jo sat in front-aisle box seats as "Ghant!" signs waved and flipped among the awestruck crowd. Then, out stepped the silver-tongued Ghant, clad in his iconic Capitalist Costume—a flawless, Italian wool, three-piece suit. The already over-stimulated audience whipped itself into a frenzy as the pompous statesman approached the podium and breathed into the microphone. Energy pulsated through the crowd. Hopped-up, they roared with maniacal glee as he now tapped on the microphone like some tender-footed amateur. But the audience did not care. It was Ghant! People were passing out from excitement in the stuffy aisles before the idol could even utter a syllable on this most glorious of evenings on the East Side of wonderful Blandon-Average.

Ghant's Dream

"Aren't I beautiful? Just look at that gorgeous face. The people adore me and they should." Ghant kissed his face in the mirror. "Beautiful, I tell you."

Phoenix's Dream

King Phoenix lay on the plush wool bedding, his female cat servants jockeying to paw-feed him hearty chunks of Ardmore Trophy White Chicken and purring in his silver ears. "No more cat food, you peons," said the exalted one. "Not for me. Never again…. Only Ardmore Trophy White Chicken."

THE I-55 EYEBALL EXCAVATOR

The smaller, older houses of west Blandon flickered by, as Elma drove home from her motel-maid job at Sparky's Paradise Inn.

The trees on this side of town stood tall and thick among the bungalows and ranch-style houses, a stark contrast to the saplings on the East side, where new houses basked in full sun along pristine streets. She soon turned onto her street, steering around the curved block. The kids, engrossed in their kickball game, scattered as she approached, waving at the friendly woman as she passed by, only to quickly regroup once she had driven through. Finally, she pulled into her narrow driveway.

Elma's attention then shifted to a radio news special: "This morning, the Chief of Police for the city of Springfield confirmed that a serial killer has been prowling the I-55 corridor in search of victims in Illinois. Chief Robert Costello reports that a total of seven bodies—all female—have been discovered along the busy expressway or on old Route 66, which often serves as a frontage road through Illinois. Two of the bodies were found in Sangamon County."

The victims have all died by strangulation according to information released by Illinois State Police and the Sangamon County Coroner. All murders have been linked to one killer. WLNK's Patricia Corning asked Roland Davis, Sangamon County Coroner, about the cause of death:

"Dr. Davis, what can you tell us about the cause of death?"

"We determined right away that strangulation had occurred in all the cases, since the Hyoid bones were broken and petechial hemorrhaging was found about the eyelids."

"What about reports that the eyeballs of the victims had been removed?"

"At this time I cannot comment on that, since that could jeopardize the investigation."

"In addition, one body was recovered near I-57 in the Shawnee National Forest and is believed to be linked to the I-55 murders.

"More information will be released as it becomes available. This is Anthony Pankiewicz, reporting. In other news, a two-car crash—"

Elma flicked off her car radio, nudging the old Honda Civic forward until it nearly touched the closed garage door. She grabbed a small sack of groceries, got out of the car, and casually strolled toward the front of the house.

As she entered her residence, the paper boy rode up and handed her the paper.

"Thank you," said Elma.

"Yes ma'am," replied the paperboy.

"Oh, could you please put a stop on the paper?"

"Sorry, ma'am. You'll have to call the office."

"OK, I'll do that."

Elma unlocked the door and tossed the paper onto the couch. She took off her shoes, went into the kitchen and set the bag of groceries on her kitchen table.

Just then, Tyrel came in. "Tyrel!" Elma half shouted.

"Yes, mom?"

"The office at school called me at work today. Who gave you permission to ditch school?"

"Ah—um."

"You're in big trouble, buster. No more band practice for a month! Now get to your room, and I'll call you for supper!"

"Mom, no. Not band prac—."

"You heard what I said, young man, now get!"

Disgusted, Elma turned on the television and switched to the evening news. After a short time, the news anchor reported on the murders.

"Authorities in Illinois now confirm that bodies have been recovered in both Illinois and Missouri. Some form of post-mortem mutilation of the eyeballs of said female victims has been reported by unnamed sources, but not confirmed. Officials remain tight-lipped about the specific nature of the mutilations, but one leak has suggested that the victims' eyeballs were removed, leading a Central Illinois news outlet to dub the killer the 'Illinois Eyeball Snatcher.' Another news source has referred to the killer as 'The I-55 Eyeball Excavator.' A press conference has been scheduled for 5 p. m. at the State Capital. In other news—."

"Oh my God," said Elma, "I can't get away from it."

OLIVER STUMBLES

The stress from Lisa's death and the agonizing funeral led Oliver astray for at least a few weeks. He started hanging out at Springfield's lowest class dive, The Warped Onion, a Bar and Grill in the seedy central part of the city. There, the still-stunned 21st Century hippie encountered characters like "Methhead" Bob, Jake "The Roach," and "Wide Load" Joan—a hard-drinking woman twice Oliver's age with a rap sheet three times the length of Jake the Roach's and Methhead Bob's combined. Despite her rough life, Joan still clung to the remnants of her sleazy-sexy days, though they were now marred by a small protruding beer gut, sagging, over-sucked breasts, and cracked, sun-baked skin.

Oliver spent one night with "Wide Load" Joan and saw right away how she had earned her nickname, as she was so stretched out, one could have parked an oversized truck in her passageway.

After three tedious weeks of this behavioral downslide, Jamelle pressed his unfortunate friend to curb his stupidity and lust and to "get your act together!"

"Oliver," Jamelle bitched, "you've got to slow down, brother. You're blowin' it, man! What about your classes? Dude, don't fuck that up!"

"Yeah, I know," the glassy-eyed hippie admitted. "I'm cool, dude. I'll get it together. Just having a hard time since Lisa's been gone."

"Yer out there screwing this ratty-assed bar hag, and people, including your mom, are starting to worry."

"I know, dude. Slap me a few times, will ya?"

But Jamelle had to have a bit of fun before they could depart. "But I do think that bartendress is hot," said the buzzed negro. "You can tell her that I got a big ol' Brontosaurus schlong that wants to do a nosedive on her banana basket!"

"Tell her yourself," replied a grinning Oliver.

"I might just do that," declared Jamelle.

"You guys are gross!" said a snickering Sally Camden, who sat at a neighboring table, and could not help but hear her friends discussing vaginas, good and bad.

"Aw, c'mon man, we're jus' havin' fun!" said Jamelle.

"Well," said a semi-tottering Sally, "what if we women went around saying stuff like 'Oh, my slobbering slit wants to come all over your sleek potato?'"

"Bring it on," invited Jamelle.

"You guys are all alike," said Sally jokingly.

The dim room was abuzz with people laughing and raising their drunken voices. But Oliver listened to his African-American friend and cut himself away from the bar scene after that night.

SPARKY'S PARADISE INN

"That's sinful," Melanie said to the stranger in the grocery store, pointing at the tattoo on his forearm—a red gargoyle with blue wings. The stranger was taken aback and didn't know how to respond.

Finally, he barked, "Mind your own business." Then he muttered "Bitch."

Meanwhile, at home, Melvin received a special phone call. It was Tug.

"Melvin," Tug's deep, raspy voice sounded through the receiver. "What's up. It's Tug."

"Tug, how are you?"

"Great. Hey, I got somethin' lined up for you."

"Wonderful," said Melvin, trying to sound calm.

"She's hot too, Melvin."

"I'll trust you, Tug."

"You gotta do it just like I say, though. No fussin' or anything."

"Why sure, Tug. Whatever you say."

"Have Melanie come to Sparky's Paradise Inn—you know where it is, up on US 150. Have her, and only her, come to Sparky's this Friday at 1 p.m. Tell her to knock on Room 209 and to bring the business card I gave you. She has to bring the card, or the girl won't go for it. And make sure she brings $300 for her services."

"Ah, OK," agreed Melvin. "We couldn't do it at the Radison or someplace like that?"

"No, it's got to be Sparky's at 1 o'clock in the afternoon on Friday, Melvin. Make sure she's alone. Room 209. OK, I gotta go. See ya!"

Click.

"What's the girl's name? Tug? Hello, Tug?"

Just as Melvin hung up and finished writing down the details, in walked Melanie with a bag of groceries.

After dinner Melvin gave her the news.

"*I'm* not going to that place!" she griped. "That place is a *dump!*"

"Now Buttercup, in any other town that motel would be a fine enough place. Yes, I admit, it is a bit low brow for Blandon-Average, but it is really not so bad."

"Maybe," said Melanie, "we should just forget the whole thing."

"No, no, dear. I made special arrangements. You have got to go. I went to all the trouble of setting it up. Now listen. You just go there at exactly 1 o'clock on Friday afternoon. It is Room 209. Ok, my little Tulip?"

"Oh, I guess. Do you think I'm doing the right thing, Melvin?"

"Yes, dear. Everything will be alright. You'll see. But you need to be at Room 209 on Friday at one o'clock p.m. And don't forget to bring Tug's business card." Melvin pulled the card from his wallet and handed it to Melanie.

"Tug? Who's that?"

"Remember Tug from that restaurant here in Blandon-Average? The big truck driver who gave me his card the day Ghant! Won the election?"

"Yeah. How did *he* get involved in this? Oh, Melvin, I don't like this."

"My little tulip, please trust me and it will be fine."

"Well, what's her name? Who do I ask for?"

"Buttercup, I didn't get a name. But it's all set up. She will open the door for you."

"What if I don't like her?"

"If you don't like her? Well, you just pay her and come back home. You don't have to do anything. Just pay her and tell her you have other plans. But you'll like her, don't worry. Tug said she's hot."

"Pay her? I don't want no prostitute!"

"She's not a prostitute, Tulip. She's an escort. Besides, I'll pay for it."

RIOTS ON MAIN STREET

Elma watched the television in astonishment and horror as the strained passages of a virulent Wackersham speech unfolded.

"The Librhoid bastards want to support drag queens!" bellowed Wackersham. "Next, they'll want to install them in the White House! Tell 'em no! Hell no! Tell 'em we'll hang the queers on the White House lawn!!!"

Elma struggled to believe that the networks were actually broadcasting Wackersham's vile tirade. Tyrell looked on, bewildered and confused.

All of the Wackersham rally sites had massive screens showing his venomous speech. Gymnasiums, cafeterias, civic centers, and arenas were all broadcasting the deranged man's message.

"These Librrhoid sonsabitches want to make everything queer! Raise hell! Tell 'em 'Up theirs.' We won't stand for it, I tell you! Take it to the streets! They'll turn your sons and daughters into queers if you let them! They're coming for you!!!"

As Wackersham's rhetoric reached its peak, crowds at all the rally sites spilled into the streets, hurling rocks and bottles at car windows and businesses. The frenzy spread to parks, where people with colored hair, long hair, spiked cuts, cornrows, or dreadlocks were attacked. The cameras eventually cut away from the violence, switching to commercials.

Elma immediately called her friend Maria. "Are you watching this?"

"Oh, my God," Maria replied. "He has really done it this time. They've all gone mad! You know, the government handed this lunatic the opportunity to stage this chaos. By not holding President Schmidt accountable for his egregious actions, they set us up for this!"

"Don't go out of the house, sweetie," Elma warned. "They're probably rioting here in Blandon-Average too."

True, a weird wave of far-right regimes had already encircled the globe over the last ten years, from Quasar to Zambonia. The worrisome trend now threatened the corruption-weary nations of North America. Like thunderous trains rolling down the main streets of America the furious throngs heaved and puffed and quaked at the stress-ridden strains of the mega-madman's spewing tirade. The gigantic theatre screens showing his mentally boiled madness at all the venues shook with a volcanic rumble. An astonishing streak of demagoguery had ignited the short-fused crowds into a revolt of mammoth proportions, crushing all inhibition, fraying every nerve ending and mutilating any sense of calm that might linger. Unbeknownst to the television viewers, mini battles had commenced. Guerilla warfare took place in the inner cities. Small groups of white rioters tangled with well-armed black resistance fighters. The ugliness of the scenes would scar America, as it became news to the world. Certain foreign leaders who despised America celebrated the chaos.

Elma checked all the locks on her windows and doors, then settled back down to see what the networks would report about the mass chaos. To her relief, the news began to broadcast reports of a calming down. As the rioters grew tired and the pandemonium subsided, Wackersham was already asleep in his bunker, cozy as a kitten on a new wool blanket. He might have been dreaming of his next violence-inciting escapade, but for now, he was enveloped in a serene quietude.

"What's happening to America?" asked a frightened Tyrel.

His mother could only sigh in utter frustration.

The next day the headline in the newspaper quoted The Peerless Profit's latest comments. In Springfield's paper it read: "Riots In Our Streets! Conservaprick Neo-Nazis Targeting Drag Queens in Effort 'to keep America from turning into one, gigantic San Francisco!' as Wackersham put it. Then, in smaller print, the article said: "Mayor of Frisco Demands Apology From Wackersham. Hate Groups Have Now Organized and are a Threat to Society."

The flaming masses trampled through the streets, killing 16 people, injuring about 3,200 and causing some $280 million in damaged property. No one of high rank was held accountable.

TWO DICKS IN SUITS

"**D**ouglas McCrea?"

"Yes."

"This is Detective Cervantes. I'm Detective Dragovich. We would like to ask you a few questions, if you don't mind, sir."

The pair of suited investigators stood on Tug's front porch and displayed their badges.

"Questions about what?" Tug's spine shook as he asked.

"Well, sir," said Detective Cervantes, "your truck was one of several sighted near a homicide scene, and we are conducting a routine investigation so as to ascertain the reason for your presence."

"Don't be alarmed, sir," said Dragovich, "we want to clear you if at all possible."

"Where was this?" asked Tug with obvious trepidation. "I'm up and down Illinois' expressways all day long. I'm a full-time driver, you know."

"Downstate Illinois," answered Cervantes. "On I-55 near Springfield...on Thursday night."

"Well, yeah, I was down there, but I sure don't know about any homicide. What makes you think that I know anything?"

"We don't know what you know," explained Detective Dragovich. "That's why we are here…to find out if you know anything."

"Well," exclaimed Tug, "I didn't kill anybody." The two detectives looked at each other with a pinch of doubt.

"We're not saying it was you, but someone gave us a partial plate number," reported Dragovich. "So, we're just doing follow-up."

"Part of the plate was identified," further explained Cervantes, "by a citizen in the proximity of the crime. And it matched yours."

"I don't know nothin' about no homicide," Tug exclaimed defensively.

"No one is accusing you of committing a crime, sir," Dragovich said. "We're just trying to determine your whereabouts and, if you were in the area, whether you saw anything and your reason for being there. We're just making sure there's no connection." Both detectives had come with an open mind, but Tug's behavior was raising suspicion.

"Don't know nothin' about it," the hulking truck driver replied. "I was on a routine run to Southern Illinois, delivering pallets of pharmaceuticals to Staunton and East St. Louis."

"Would you be willing to take a polygraph test?" inquired Cervantes, now highly intrigued by Tug's defensive demeanor.

"Ah, no—I think we're at a point where I need to talk to my lawyer."

"Fair enough, sir," said Cervantes. "We'll be talking again."

Tug shut the front door gently, as he realized he may have seemed suspicious. He went back to admiring his Matchbox cars, only he could not much concentrate, for his mind ran like a fast brook. This experience rendered the big man extremely nervous. He said to himself, those sons-a-bitches have nothing. But they're on to me. Goddamnit, they're on to me. Shit, I have nothing to hide. Oh fuck, am I in for it. Back and forth he went through the tense afternoon.

But when the moon flashed its yellowy light upon the somber evening, the hours began to crawl the way a caterpillar inches up a tree. By ten o'clock in the evening, he said to himself, Tug, you're a nervous wreck. I know, I know. Settle down, man. Settle down.

The wretched minutes dragged by tediously, yet he could not keep his mind from racing like a wolf spider across a polished kitchen floor. And the sleepless night crept on with stark terror.

Every so often, Tug drifted into a light sleep, only to wake, check the Ghant! Sign in his front yard through the window, and reassure himself that everything would be alright. When he finally glanced at the clock and saw it was 1:00 a.m., he threw off the covers, got up, slipped into his trousers, grabbed the keys to his old Cadillac, and, leaving through the side door of his spacious apartment, set off for an early morning drive. He cruised down Milwaukee Avenue until he spotted a small group of people outside Smoky's Tap.

"They'll never catch me," he said aloud. "They're just a couple of boneheaded cops." Despite his bravado, his already strained nerves caused him physical pain. An old injury in his arm, where his father had struck him with a two-by-four, began to throb. He knew this usually happened when he felt upset or anxious about something.

SHABBY TABBY

Tug contemplated fleeing the state and commencing a new life. He launched a pint of whiskey and bit his fingernails for a time. He grew so agitated that he developed diarrhea. Upon exhausting himself at a truckstop toilet, he felt improvement in his physical being.

Tug, feeling increasingly restless and reckless, pulled up to the small group gathered in the parking lot of the tavern. "Anybody need a ride?" he called out as he rolled down his window.

To his surprise, a disheveled girl with frizzy blonde hair and blue eyes answered, "Yo, I need a ride!" Despite her friends' warnings, she climbed into the passenger seat when Tug opened the door. "Can you take me up to Cicero Avenue and I-290?"

"I think I can manage that," Tug replied.

As he pulled out of the parking lot, he asked, "So what's your name? I'm Tug."

"You ain't gonna try to pull nothin' on me, are ya?" she asked, her pupils dilated. "I'm Tabitha. My friends just call me Tabby."

"You're safe and sound with me, Tabby," Tug said with a forced smile. "You work there or just live there?"

"Neither. I'm going to see a friend. Ain't nothin' but whores up there, but I ain't no workin' girl."

Tug saw this as an opportunity, sensing that Tabby, though she might appear to be a working girl, was not one. He soon merged onto I-290 and headed toward Chicago. "So, are you just out partying?" he asked.

"Pretty much. I left my three kids with my mom tonight, so I'm just trippin' out and havin' a good time of it."

"Well, we could go out partying if you'd like. I'm buyin'."

"I apprec'ate the offer, but I gotta meet somebody."

Before 2:00 am Tug exited the freeway onto South Cicero Avenue. "This is a pretty seedy area, don't you think, Tabby?" With that, Tug pulled into an old motel.

"What're you doing?" protested Tabby. "I didn't tell you to turn in here."

"Just stoppin' here to pee," said Tug. He pulled up to the back of the dingy sleeping place, put the car in park, and left the engine running.

"Well, make it quick," ordered the sassy mistress. "I gotta meet somebody."

Tug, in a state of frenzy, grabbed the bitchy blonde by the hair and stuck his hand over her mouth. "Fuck with me, bitch, and your life is over." Tug figured her life was over anyway one could look at it, so he moved his hand from her mouth to her throat, not even bothering to put on his shirt, mask or gloves. Tabby scratched his cheeks, then gouged his left eye. "Oh, you fucking cunt, I'll rip your heart out for that!"

Tabby proved a wild one, wilder than Tug could have imagined. She elbowed him in the crotch, clawed his arms, and slithered away, while opening the car door. The big man punched her, though he could not gather much leverage inside the car. Suddenly, Tabby jumped out, yelling and screeching her way through the dark parking lot. Tug considered giving chase to the wicked wench, but he decided otherwise, putting the big car in gear, pulling backward, and peeling fresh rubber on the broken-up lot. Soon, he raced up Cicero, veered onto the expressway and tore out of one of Chicago's most notorious neighborhoods.

"Fuck!" he yelled. "Those mother fucker's will be all over me tomorrow! God Damnit to hell! I fucked up!"

Completely wired, Tug swerved through the streets of Wheeling, Illinois. He had just blown the chance he had waited so long for, to strangle a non-prostitute. When he reached his apartment, he pulled around to the alley and tried to hide the Cadillac as best he could. But the tormented serial killer could not reel-in his madly swimming mind. He drew in a heavy breath, exhaled and tried to settle down. After a moment he got out of the car. When Tug went to let himself in, he noticed a business card attached to his front door. It read, "Oscar Popadopolis, FBI Agent." Tug was stunned. Overcome by a surge of paranoia, he rushed inside and began packing his clothes. After he finished, he downed another pint of whiskey and collapsed onto his bed, slipping into a stupor until morning. He knew that since one of his victims had been found in Missouri, the FBI had taken on the case due to their interstate crime policy.

The huge man snored loudly as the early morning hours wore away.

BOTH FEET IN

"Tyrel, your shirts and underwear are not folded correctly, son," admonished Elma. "You have got to fold them so that one end does not overlap the other end. Now please refold these the right way."

"Yes, mom," Tyrel replied, "but don't you think that is being a little picky?"

"Just do as I say, son, and we will have no problems."

"Ok, mom."

"Now mom has got to work on Friday, Tyrel. But do not forget, no band practice. If you behave, maybe I will cut your punishment in half—only two weeks instead of a month of no band practice."

"Yes, mom."

"I'm going to check up on you," Elma assured the young musician. "Don't let your mother down."

Elma wetted a piece of toilet paper and wiped a green mouthwash stain from the top of the bathroom sink. She then flushed the toilet with her right foot. Once the water disappeared in the bowl, and the tank filled up, she flushed the toilet again with her left foot, even though it did not need it. Then, she walked out to the living room. Next, Elma turned on the Springfield news and listened to the latest on what they now called "The Case of The Illinois Eye Digger." She waited a moment, while the newscast went into its silly, obligatory, feel-good fluff stories, and then a few commercials. Finally, just before the newscast ended, they gave one last heads-up regarding the serial killer.

"Women are watching over their shoulders and locking their doors tonight as an apparent serial killer wreaks havoc across the state. As of yesterday, six bodies are attributed to the so-called Illinois Eye Digger, and law enforcement fears there are more yet to be discovered. The latest victim was found in a cornfield in rural Blandon-Average at about 6 p.m. on Wednesday. Investigators have isolated DNA from some of the crime scenes but have come up empty when cross-checking criminal databases. We'll have more on this story later. WTNV News, Springfield."

"Oh dear," sighed Elma, "I don't like hearing horrible news like that."

She walked into the kitchen to make some tea, stepping carefully on the lines between the tiles. She had to step on each line an equal number of times with each foot. If she stepped on a line three times with her right foot and only two times with her left, it would itch at her, much like a secret that gnaws at one's resolve to keep it hidden. She couldn't bear the thought of this imbalance.

Her doctor had told her to begin her withdrawal from this addiction, so he prescribed medicine and then told her to first give up these trivial acts. So, she had purposely stepped on a line one extra time with her right foot. Now she sat down in the living room with her tea but could hardly bear the agony of having stepped on the line one extra time with her right foot.

Meanwhile, the newsman went on with more shallow feel-good stories until he made an abrupt announcement. "This story just breaking," the voice on the television set said. "Apparently, police are questioning a woman who was attacked but who survived what might be the serial killer last night. They say that a woman was choked and beaten Thursday night on Cicero Avenue near the I-290 interchange, but she managed to escape. The woman has come forward and has allegedly identified the suspect. Police are withholding the name at this time. More on this story at 10:00 o'clock."

Finally, a nervous Elma got up and walked to the threshold of the kitchen and placed her left foot on a line, then turned and sat down again. For a moment, she felt whole.

SADIE COMES TO PLAY (SERIAL KILLER MEETS SERIAL KILLER)

One rosy evening, Tug, still yearning to branch out to darker-skinned females, got hold of a bad date. He phoned Sadie Alberghetti on a tip he had gotten from his main source. Sadie was wanted for four separate murders in the Akron, Ohio area, but, of course, Tug was unaware.

Tug picked up the Italian maiden at Ivan's Roadhouse outside of Marion, Illinois. He parked his rig behind the adjoining Aladdin Motel. Tug lured her to the back of the cab and paid her $150. Sadie had deep-black frizzy hair, a medium-to-dark skin tone, and a mole on her left cheek.

"By the way, I'm Sadie," said the thin woman with large brown eyes.

"I'm Tug."

"I ain't no whore at all, you see," said the tough-looking but strangely sexy date. "I jus' need the money real bad. So, whatcha got fer me, big daddy?"

"Oh, a tough one, eh?" joked the big man.

"Damn right. I sliced up four men."

"You shit."

"I don't give two flyin' fucks if you believe me or not. So, I'll ask you again. Whatcha got fer me, big daddy? You think you can get it on?"

"I got two big hands around your neck, skinny." Tug's ornery fingers, as thick as broomsticks, wrapped themselves around the bad girl's throat. But no quicker did Tug tighten his grip then he felt a sudden, intense, stinging pain in his shoulder.

"Ahhhhhh!" he yelled, as he let go of the olive-skinned, one-night hussy. Sadie had pulled a knife from her purse and slashed his flesh before pulling away the blade.

"I'll cut yer stinkin' fat balls off, you two-ton bitch!" the hardened woman belted out. "Now get the fuck offa me!"

"What'd you do to me, you ignorant cunt!"

"Back off, or I'll slice you again!" Tug did back off. Then, he pulled his own knife from the sheath on his tool belt, though he did not move forward.

Now Tug had blood in his cab, but it was his own. He quickly stood up, blood streaming down his arm, and grabbed Sadie's wrist before she could stab him again. After dropping his knife, he lifted the wildcat from the bed and threw her against the center console in the front of the cab. "Owwww!" she yelled, clutching her neck. She quickly recovered and screamed, "C'mon you bloated hick! Come at me again and I'll gouge your fat eyes out!" Sadie rubbed her neck with her free hand and took a few swipes in the air with her knife-wielding hand. "I'll butcher your fat ass and lay you out like a roasted hog!"

"Just try it, bitch!" hollered the massive driver, pressing on his wound and picking up his knife from the blue carpet.

Medusa and her head of snakes couldn't have rivaled the hideous stare Sadie directed at Tug. Behind her brown eyes burned with flames of pure malice. Her pupils cut like lasers into Tug's shrinking bravado. Just as he felt his knees beginning to buckle, he saw the devilish hag reaching for the cab door. But she had one more venomous remark to spit his way.

"You bloated orangutan, I'll slice you up like a tomato!" And she meant it, having slain all four of her previous victims with that same knife.

"Get out of here!" yelled the stunned trucker. Sadie reintroduced Tug to fear, perhaps for the first time since his deceased father last beat him.

Now he wrapped his arm cautiously with a fresh white T-shirt, while not taking his eyes off of the ornery woman. He could smell her anger, as if it bled from her pores. She gritted her teeth and curled one side of her upper lip. Finally, she scrambled for the door of the cab and let herself out. The standoff was over. Sadie got away with the $150.

"I won't kill you if you won't kill me," Tug muttered half-jokingly in an effort to muffle the humiliation he felt at his sudden re-acquaintance with fear.

Tug finished wrapping his arm with the T-shirt, put his truck in gear, and soon headed for the emergency room. He needed thirty-two stitches to close the laceration on his bulky shoulder. The next day, Tug read about the wanted Sadie in a Chicago newspaper. Seething with anger, he punched another hole in the wall, but this time it was the wall of his cab.

MINACIOUS PROPOSALS

Ghant Wackersham made the usual boring State of the Union address on television. Afterwards, he called for special attention of viewers and made some alarming proposals to Congress.

"Friends, neighbors, ladies and gentlemen of the House and Senate, America has gone through some trying times of late. The proposals laid out by Wackersham were extreme, suggesting invasive measures and draconian laws that would severely impact personal freedoms and privacy. The notion of recording every newborn's DNA, inserting micro-chips into all citizens, and imposing mandatory church attendance was starkly oppressive. His call for segregation of intersex people, gays, and lesbians, along with random lie detector tests and urine samples for minors, was blatantly discriminatory.

The most alarming part was the suggestion of making the office of the President all-powerful and the possible implementation of martial law, reflecting an authoritarian vision.

Despite the severity of these proposals, they were met with applause from a small group of Senators who were eager to align themselves with Wackersham's rhetoric. Their support, marked by their sycophantic behavior, showed how deeply ingrained their political ambitions were, even at the expense of democratic values and human rights. The image of these Senators clinging to Wackersham's ideas highlighted a troubling trend of political opportunism and moral compromise.

And a fresh wave of fascist sympathy manifested itself in the onlookers of the strange affair, as if America had grown weary of the scuffles and battles to preserve democracy. The infectious bent for tight control by government entities left some sickened, while others simply yawned. This inert attitude perhaps embodied the most frightening aspect of the entire Wackersham odyssey. One could almost hear the whispers among the somnambulant masses: "Let Democracy be. It will fix itself."

Of course, Oliver and his cohorts were horrified. So too was the liberal media. Calls for immediate impeachment—Wackersham's fourth—bounced through the halls and caverns of Washington D. C. and even the Pentagon. The House of Representatives had enough Librhoid votes to prevent any such lunacy from becoming law, but the Senate had enough Conservaprick votes to thwart impeachment. Yet the panic of those who cared reached mountainous levels.

● ● ●

Finally, after years of waiting, former President Schmidt was indicted. The indictments came in waves, and there were 91 counts in all. The Protectors of Legacy thought they could stall it until it would just go away, as people forgot about it. But it did not go away. Schmidt would not die, and the Librhoids, for once, pressed the issue and showed some strength.

But Oliver had something to say about it: "They can pile on the indictments, the crooked deal revelations, and the rape charges all they desire, but it is only one man. Besides, if convicted, he will just get pardoned by the next president anyway. Moreover, there have always been power-starved nuts seeking top governmental offices. Some succeed; some do not. But what are we going to do about the sixty million plus nuts who elected Schmidt and then Wackersham? That is the real problem. You cannot arrest them. You cannot deem them all insane and incompetent to vote. You cannot segregate them. What the hell can we do?"

IN A SNAP

Tug dreamed of bad things. His life was in shambles. He had the County Police, State Police and FBI watching for him. If Tug was a fastidious necrophilic sadist in his "normal" life, he was now a raging, reckless, flame-throwing, flashing-red-light terrorist in his new life. A wild man among wild men. His ultra-psychotic behavior reflected his desperate condition.

Tug's urgent departure from Chicago signaled a desperate attempt to evade the mounting scrutiny from the FBI. His decision to leave behind his belongings, including the few furnishings he owned, demonstrated the gravity of his situation. The hurried packing and flight to The Safari Motel were driven by a clear intention to distance himself from the city and its increasingly tense atmosphere.

As he drove south, the Cadillac carrying his essential items and Matchbox Car collection, Tug's mind was preoccupied with his next move. The choice to forgo a shower and head straight to the trucking office underscored his urgency. The transition to his rig and the subsequent drive down I-57 toward Southern Illinois marked the beginning of his escape plan.

Despite the stress of the situation, Tug's disturbing desire for violence persisted. His yearning for another victim revealed a dark, underlying impulse that he struggled to control. This inner conflict added a layer of tension to his already precarious situation, as he sought to evade the law while grappling with his own violent tendencies.

After about two and one-half hours of driving, he called his next date from the highway.

"Hello, Carmen?"

"Yes, this is Ca'mon speaking, what can I do for ya?"

"This is Tug. I'm a first timer. Hey, how much for an all-nighter?"

"Well, you can have me for the night for $500."

"That's kind of steep, don't you think?"

"I'll tell you what, I'll do it for you for $450. That's as low as I can go. Gotta pay rent, you know."

"OK. Where are you?"

"You know where the old Bel-Aire Motel is at in Effingham, Illinois?"

"Yeah, can I pick you up in a half hour? I'm up near Neoga right now."

"Sounds good. I'll be waiting out in front. You can pok' yer ca' on the side. I gotta have cash up front, though."

"No problem. Hey, we're going to be driving to Southern Illinois in a truck, if that's ok."

"If yer payin', I'm layin'. See you in a half hour."

The truck's rumbling engines and the blaring hillbilly music created a constant, almost deafening backdrop as it roared down the I-57 toward Cairo, Illinois. The sky above was gradually darkening, with the first stars beginning to appear against the twilight canvas. The massive rig's headlights pierced through the encroaching night, their beams cutting across the trees that lined the highway in a continuous blur.

Tug's guest, sitting silently beside him, gazed out the window. The landscape beyond was an indistinct wash of shadows and fleeting glimpses of foliage, punctuated only by the distant, rhythmic blinking of a solitary red tower light. The guest's mind seemed far removed from the physical surroundings, lost in their own thoughts as the truck sped toward its destination. The combination of the truck's relentless movement and the eerie quiet of the night created a tense atmosphere, hinting at the gravity of the journey they were on.

The good old strands of Clayton Crawdad and His Hillbilly Crooners drenched the soundwaves inside the rig. Carmen glanced at the CD case on the console.

"What's wrong?" asked Tug as he turned down the music.

"Who the hell ah *these* guys?" asked Carmen.

"Why that's Clayton Crawdad and His Hillbilly Crooners. It's 70s music. Stuff you're unfamiliar with, I'm sure."

Carmen squawked, "It sounds like Clayton Crawdad and His Stinky Bottle o' Piss, if you want my opinion." Tug said nothing, but immediately jacked the music up again. The shadows of the evening crept in and the highway view dimmed. The unlikely pair of riders seemed a thousand miles apart.

Finally, the big man turned the country music down, when, seemingly out of nothingness, a most amazing incident happened. Some giant boat hovered above the laboring truck. It was a Thursday night, but the traffic was thin. The thing stayed just ahead of the blue truck. The cab-weary pair looked up in stark astonishment. The gargantuan ship, which dwarfed the truck, had three lights underneath, two red lights near the back and one green light near the front. The thing just hung there with its classic cigar-shaped body and its soundless presence overwhelming the couple. It lingered there for a moment, then darted off into the starry heavens with a speed like light and unlike any speed ever attained by any earth-made machine.

"Gallopin' grandmothers!" blurted Tug, "what the hell was that? Did you see that thing?"

"I sawr it," replied Carmen, her blood-shot eyes larger than a pair of ping-pong balls.

"I—I can't believe it! Am I dreaming...."

"You ain't dreamin', hon', I sawr it too!"

Carmen laid her bony hand on Tug's knee. "I am totally freaked," she exclaimed. The moonlight showed the bags under her eyes, a long, thin nose, and the smoker's wrinkles around her lips. "I wonda if any other ca's seen it?"

Carmen's East Coast accent, thick and vibrant even in the midst of tension, cut through the hum of the truck's engine. "That was a giant spaceship!" she exclaimed, her voice tinged with disbelief and excitement.

Tug, who had been nervously laughing, now coasted the truck onto the shoulder of the highway, his laughter subsiding into a tense silence. He glanced over at Carmen, his face a mix of anxiety and curiosity. "I mean, what else could it have been?!" he asked, his voice cracking slightly.

He shook his head in frustration, grappling with the surreal experience. "You think we should report it?" he added, clearly uncertain. The notion of reporting such an outlandish sight seemed almost absurd, yet the unease in his gut suggested that it might be worth investigating.

"I ain't reportin' that thing," squawked Carmen. "No one'd believe us anyway. They'd haul us to the looney bin!"

Tug gradually pulled to a stop along the side of the lonely highway. He put the truck in park and wiped the perspiration from his forehead. Then Tug grabbed the girl by the neck and tried to squeeze it like a fresh orange, but his grip was not tight, weakened by perspiration on his hands, and the slinky middle-aged woman wrestled out of it. "What the fuck-a you doin', you sick sonofabitch?" shouted the skinny tart. Then she opened the rig's door and jumped out. Landing on her wrist, she broke it on the hard asphalt and gravel shoulder of the road. "Ah!" she screamed. Then, as Tug let himself out of his side, she scrambled to her feet and ran for the woods.

Carmen was a bit quicker than Tug, as she slid into the ditch on the side of the road, and scampered up the other side of it. Tug took it a little slower, but soon pulled himself up the other side and ran with all of his might. Suddenly, Carmen, who ran well ahead of Tug, smashed into a tree and instantly collapsed to the ground at the edge of the forest. Tug reached her and fell onto her, and, breathing heavily, grabbed her again by the neck. He was about to slug Carmen in the face when he saw how mangled her face already was from slamming it into the tree.

"You got fucked up, didn't you?" laughed the brawny trucker.

"Please don't hurt me no more." Carmen begged. "I think I broke my wrist...and my jaw hurts. Please, I--I'm in bad shape."

"I don't care about your damn wrist," the enormous man yelled. With that, he grabbed hold of Carmen's other arm, applied his knee just below her elbow, and pulled on her wrist until the forearm snapped like a dry branch.

"Ah! Owwwww! Oh, my God, please, no more!" Her face contorted with the pain and terror of the moment. She was now basically armless. "Please don't. I'll have sex with you for free, whatever you want! I'll give you your money back!" She writhed in pain for a moment, then paused to gather her senses. "Please don't hurt me no more!" she moaned, out of breath and broken. "I have two kids, a boy and a little girl. Please!" Tug stared down at her with slanted, mean eyes. She sighed, "We have something between us, you know," she reasoned desperately. "We both sawr the spaceship. Please let me go. I won't tell."

Tug thought about it for a moment, then he realized that he did not bring his quiver full of stick-swords. Now he reached into Carmen's bra, where she had stashed the wad of folded dollar bills, took the money and stuffed it in his shirt pocket. "OK, bitch. I'll let you go, BUT NOT 'CAUSE I FEEL SORRY FOR YOU OR ANYTHING! Let me tell you, if you say anything to the cops about this, I will hunt you down and mangle every bone in your miserable body. Do you understand?"

"Yes!" cried Carmen. "Oh, thank you, thank you! Oh, my God, it hurts!"

Tug picked himself up off the grass and told the girl to "shut up for a moment. I got to make a call." Carmen just whimpered lightly as the burly driver took his phone out of his pocket. He then dug a piece of paper out of his other pants pocket, snatched a flashlight from his tool belt and shined it on the paper. Finally, he dialed the number on his cellphone.

"Thomas's Discount Wholesale," said a phony-sounding voice. "What kind of deal can I make with you today?"

"Yeah," Tug calmly said, "they were supposed to send someone out to repair my mom's washing machine, but they never showed up."

"I'm so sorry, sir. What was your mom's address?" Tug turned away from the sprawled-out and moaning Carmen and began walking back to his truck. "Hold on a second..." he said, and walked until he was out of earshot from his victim. "The address," he whispered, "is 235 Cherry St., Chicago, Illinois. Can you send someone out tomorrow?" "Yes, yes," said the salesman. "Between noon and four o'clock OK? They'll call before they come, of course." Tug agreed with the time and ended the call. He left behind the terror-stricken prostitute and never saw her again.

As Tug walked back to his truck, he cast one last glance at Carmen, who lay on the grass, her suffering palpable. The phone call had been a distraction, a way to distance himself from the grim reality of his actions. He climbed into his truck, started the engine, and drove away, leaving Carmen behind in the cold, dark night.

Carmen, in immense pain and desperation, managed to pull herself together after Tug had left. With her arms severely injured and barely able to function, she used her feet to knock on the farmhouse door. Her knocks were weak but persistent, a desperate call for help.

The door opened to reveal a startled homeowner, who quickly assessed the dire situation. Carmen, barely able to speak through her pain, managed to explain the gravity of her injuries and the need for immediate medical attention. The homeowner, shaken but composed, called emergency services, and Carmen was soon on her way to receive the care she desperately needed.

UN-RAPPING THINE EVIL

Tug got tied up in Southern Illinois by being overweight with his load, so he arrived in Springfield on Friday instead of Thursday. He had called Mandy Jo on Thursday night to notify her. However, it being Friday, he wanted to make it to Blandon by about 12:30 in the afternoon and then roll into the Chicago Metro area of Illinois by 4:00 pm..

As the blistering sun beat down over the sprawling corn and soy fields of Illinois, Elma started her day with her usual routine. Having left for work at 8:00 am, she arrived at Sparky's Paradise Inn and began her shift. The tenants, some of whom looked worn and ragged from their travels, began checking out as expected.

By 8:30 am, Elma was ready to dive into her daily room-cleaning assignments. She pushed her cleaning cart down the worn corridors of the inn, her steps steady and practiced. The sun's oppressive heat outside contrasted sharply with the cooler, shaded interior of the inn, offering a brief escape from the relentless summer blaze.

She could also periodically check in on Tyrel, as he had earned his way into such strict monitoring.

Meanwhile, back in Springfield, Tug, in heading back to the Chicago area, had pulled his big truck into the empty lot next to Mandy Jo's house and tooted ever so lightly on the bold horn. Out came Mandy in her summer garb, blue shorts and a light-yellow T-shirt.

Mandy was talking to the mailman in her front yard, when Tug received a call from his mother. "Tuggy, dear," Mrs McRae said in an alarmed tone, "they have got yellow tape around your apartment building and they're doing something inside!"

Tug groaned, "It's probably a search warrant, mom."

"What on earth—."

Tug cut his mother off, as Mandy Jo approached the truck. He then turned the phone off. He felt highly aggravated, but tried his mightiest to conceal it. Finally, he opened the passenger door for Mandy Jo. Oliver had walked Mandy Jo out to the lot where Tug was parked. Oliver saw something peculiar and, frankly, kind of haunting.

Tug's face bore the fresh marks of his recent struggles, with open scratches marring his rugged features. His arm, wrapped in bandages, was a testament to the violent encounters he had endured. The relentless pressure from law enforcement had taken a toll on him, leaving him both physically and mentally strained.

As he drove, his focus was not just on the road but also on his urgent need to maintain a facade of normalcy. "If you don't mind, doll," Tug said to his passenger, "I've got to stop off at Sparky's Motel before I head up to Morris. I gotta meet somebody about some business at one o'clock."

You can jus' wait in the truck, if that's OK. I'll leave it running, so you'll have music and air conditioning."

All of this time Mandy Jo stared at Tug with an incredulous open-mouthed demeanor. "My God," she exclaimed, "what happened to your face?"

"Aw, I just had a little accident the other day," explained Tug. "While mowing the lawn for my mom, I ran into some dead branches. I'll be OK."

"Geez oh mighty, it looks like a wildcat got a hold of you!"

"It's alright, really."

"And you're arm too! Oh, my Lord!" A small spot of blood showed through Tug's bandaged limb.

"Yeah, I did that while unloading at the warehouse," Tug lied yet again.

"You look shaken," said Mandy Jo. "Are you sure you're alright?"

"Really. I'm fine." Tug lied. "Let's go have a nice trip."

"Well, ok, if you're sure you're alright," said a gullible Mandy Jo.

Then Tug announced: "There's been a change in plans, though. We're going to skip Joliet. We'll head up to Berwyn, Illinois, grab our load, and start heading toward Southern Illinois tonight. I can't go home…on account that they're painting. Can't stand the smell, you know. If you get tired, you can sleep in the back of the truck, while I drive."

Soon they rambled up I-55 to Blandon-Average, then rolled up to Sparky's Paradise Inn, where Tug found a few empty parking spaces and pulled in. The colossal truck's air brakes hissed and the engine was set to idling.

"I got the air on fer you," the big man said, while grabbing two sticks from his quiver hanging behind his seat. Now he lifted his enormous body from the seat and climbed down onto an asphalt parking lot, so hot that the surface was slightly bleeding tar. Mandy Jo could only see the top of Tug's swollen head.

"What're those sticks for?" asked a curious Mandy Jo.

"Oh. Well, you just never mind," warned Tug. "I'll be back in a few."

He was just a little early, so he found another semi-truck in the lot and, in the full sun of the day, stealthily stole its license plate. Then he went back to his own truck and changed his plate to the stolen plate.

As Tug adjusted the stolen license plate on his truck, his movements were quick and deliberate. The hot asphalt of the parking lot seemed to ripple under the sun's intensity, but he remained focused on his task. After disposing of his old plate and ensuring his new one was securely attached, he made his way into the lobby of Sparky's Paradise Inn.

The air-conditioned interior of the motel was a welcome relief from the sweltering heat outside. Tug walked up to the front desk, his appearance somewhat incongruous with the casual nature of the establishment. He kept his gaze low, avoiding eye contact with the receptionist, and checked in under an alias to avoid drawing attention.

Outside, Melanie Goodall drove down Market Street, her eyes scanning for the familiar sign of Sparky's Paradise Inn. Upon spotting it, she pulled into the lot with purpose. Melanie had a reason for her visit—one that might intersect with Tug's plans. She parked her car and made her way toward the entrance, unaware of the complexities unfolding just inside the motel.

As Melanie approached the front desk, she caught sight of Tug from behind, his back turned to her as he completed his check-in. The encounter could lead to unexpected developments, given the secrecy and tension that surrounded Tug's current situation.

"I don't believe I'm doing this," she muttered, as she walked toward the front door.

While she walked delicately through the lobby and pressed the button for the elevator, Melanie noticed an African-American kid listening to headphones and holding what clearly appeared as a rap CD. She could see an overconfident, muscular black man with tattoos on the cover of the CD. She could hear the incessant thumping bass line and the dreaded, cocky, monotone voice. Being afraid of black people, she tried desperately to refrain from commenting. Finally, no longer able to fend off the urge to speak, she tapped the young man on the shoulder. He removed one side of the headphones just as the elevator door opened, and Melanie said to the boy in a shaky tone, "I'll pray for your salvation."

The young man grimaced and gave Melanie a what-the-fuck look, then, allowing the headphone to snap back in place over his ear, followed her into the crowded elevator. The Spongez conservative was quite nervous at this moment and felt as though she might turn around and go back home, but when the bell on the elevator sounded and the doors opened, she stepped timidly onto the second floor.

"Lord, be with me," she whispered, as she approached Room 209.

Meanwhile, a suspicious Oliver, his friend, Jamelle, and Phoenix had followed Tug and Mandy Jo all the way from Springfield, and they parked across the street from the motel. "What in the hell are they doing?" Oliver wondered aloud. While waiting for Tug to exit the motel, Oliver dabbled in philosophy. "I have a theory about the art of dealing with death," he told Jamelle. Phoenix yawned as if to prepare himself for one of Oliver's long, deep analyses.

Oliver's words hung in the air, a heavy reminder of the existential fears that drove human behavior. He leaned against the counter, his face a mix of weariness and intensity as he spoke. His observations about the lengths to which people would go to confront their fear of death seemed to resonate with his own experiences and the darkness he grappled with.

Jamelle, who had been listening attentively, offered a different perspective. "Well," he said, his tone thoughtful, "I believe in something after death, even if it's not the celebrated heaven that most people believe in. To me, it's more about finding meaning and connection in whatever comes next, rather than clinging to specific doctrines."

Oliver glanced at Jamelle, considering his response. "That's an interesting viewpoint," he said slowly. "Maybe it's easier to find comfort in some form of continuity, whether it's through belief or personal philosophy. But what about the ones who don't find that kind of solace? The ones who face their fear head-on without any framework to support them?"

Jamelle nodded, understanding the complexity of the situation. "For some, that's where the real struggle lies. It's a personal journey to find meaning, and not everyone has the same path or the same tools to deal with it. Some turn to religion, some to science, and some to their own personal beliefs or experiences."

Oliver sighed, his mind shifting back to the task at hand. "I suppose we all find our own way to make sense of things. Anyway, let's not get too philosophical about it. I've got business to attend to."

I mean, maybe death is like sleeping for eternity? Maybe it's all like one long dream."

"I'd doubt it," said Oliver confidently, "it's not like sleeping. It's like nothing. It's like before you were born; consciousness doesn't exist. When you sleep, you dream; when you die, you don't dream. It's non-existence. Death is the great equalizer, Jamelle; the kings, the pharaohs, the business moguls all have nothing on you or I. When death comes a-tapping on their window sills, they're reduced to the same dust as us. No more high ranking; no more exalted presence. Just dust. In fact, they have nothing on that drabby hobo we always see on the streets of downtown Springfield."

"Well dude," responded Jamelle, "for you, that may be true. But for me...well, I just have something else in mind."

"Yeah," noted Oliver, "people don't like it when you say death is nothingness. They criticize you, scowl at you, ostracize you. Do not try to shatter their hope."

"You mean like you just shattered mine?" complained Jamelle.

"Sorry, dude," apologized Oliver. "Think whatever you are comfortable with. Pay me no mind."

The tension began to boil like the soup in a campfire kettle. The whole world seemed a-flame with insanity.

RENDEZVOUS

Melanie tapped lightly on the heavy door. She felt as though her bowels would jump through her throat and out of her mouth. She looked up and down the silent hallway and shuddered. Suddenly, the door burst open and a giant hand grabbed Melanie by the hair and neck. A colossal man in a ski mask pulled her part way into the room. Her shriek was cut off by a large, gloved hand over her mouth, but Elma Ray, who had just gotten off the elevator with her housekeeping utensils, heard the scuffle, immediately grabbed her push broom and ran toward the sound.

Melanie had managed to keep the door ajar with her right foot. She fought a gallant battle with the hulking stranger, using all the strength she could muster to keep him from having his way. She finally freed a hand and ripped off the ski mask and was shocked to see a vaguely familiar face with multiple scratches. She bit one of his fingers and scratched his face anew, as she realized it was Tug, the big truck driver Melvin and she had met at the restaurant in Blandon a month before. Just then Elma pushed the door open and clobbered Tug with the wide end of her push broom.

Melanie broke free and ran toward the Exit, screeching like a wild sample of Jimi Hendrix' feedback. Elma, a pretty sizeable creature herself, continued to batter Tug, who had his arms up in self-defense and was grunting like a mad bull.

Upon seeing the frightened and battered Melanie run outside, Oliver and Jamelle jumped out of the car and ran to her aid. Oliver quickly suspected that Tug had something to do with the incident. Mandy Jo was shocked to see her son and his friend, while Oliver yelled and waved for her to get out of the truck and go to the car. But she just sat in the passenger seat of the big rig. Outside Melanie kept screaming and crying, while Oliver and Jamelle tried their best to allay her fears, so she could tell them what had occurred to make her so hysterical.

"He--attacked me—a man attacked me! Please help!" cried Melanie. "He's coming for me!"

Jamelle dialed 911 on his cell phone. He explained to the 911 operator what had so far transpired at the infamous Sparky's. Then, they all walked toward the idling semi-truck on the side lot, Oliver holding onto Melanie. But, to their brain-scorching shock, Tug burst through the exit door and barreled toward them. Melanie ran for the gas station across the street, shrieking like an injured child. Then, out the same door came Elma with her broom cocked over her shoulder. Tug turned around and ducked Elma's swipe with the broom, then he slugged her directly in the nose. Elma staggered back and fell to the ground. Now Tug ran to his truck, opened the door, and while a frightened Mandy Jo jumped out the other side, he climbed in with real athletic prowess for such a large man. Quickly, he grabbed one of his duel-edged sticks from the quiver he had hanging in the truck, while Mandy Jo stood outside the truck, motionless and paralyzed with fear. Tug jumped down from the cab and commenced a kind of sword fight with Elma.

As the chaotic scene unfolded, Oliver, Mandy Jo, and Jamelle found themselves paralyzed by the intensity of the moment. Melanie, now safely across the street, continued to scream for help, her cries echoing across the parking lot. Tug's actions had transformed what was meant to be a routine stop into a frenzied battle.

Oliver, his eyes wide with disbelief, shouted again, "What the hell are you doing?" His voice was filled with desperation and frustration, but Tug seemed completely absorbed in his bizarre duel with Elma. The trucker's movements were swift and aggressive, his duel-edged stick clashing with Elma's broom in a display of raw physicality.

Elma, despite her obvious pain, was not backing down. Her fierce determination was evident as she parried Tug's attacks with the broom, her movements surprisingly agile for someone in her condition. Blood from her nose smeared across her face, adding to the grim spectacle.

Mandy Jo, still frozen in fear, watched in horror as the two combatants clashed. The surreal nature of the fight seemed almost theatrical in its absurdity. Tug's heavy-set figure lunged forward with the stick, while Elma used the broom to fend off his advances. It was clear that neither was willing to yield.

Jamelle, having ended the call with 911, rushed to Elma's side, trying to offer some form of assistance. He shouted at Tug, trying to get his attention and perhaps redirect the man's aggression. "Stop this! What are you doing? There are people here who need help!"

But Tug's focus remained solely on Elma. The scene was becoming increasingly chaotic, with the sound of clashing weapons, shouting voices, and the constant wail of Melanie's cries blending into a cacophony of confusion and fear.

Oliver, taking a deep breath, grabbed a nearby metal pipe from the truck lot and moved towards Tug, hoping to intervene before the situation escalated further. He knew that something had to be done to stop the madness and ensure that everyone, including Elma and Melanie, could be safe from the enraged trucker.

As Oliver approached, Jamelle tried to calm Elma and assess her injuries, doing his best to protect her from further harm. The urgency of the situation weighed heavily on everyone, and it was clear that the arrival of law enforcement couldn't come soon enough.

He missed but managed to hit Elma again with his fist, this time in the mouth. But the blow did not fully connect, as she bobbed up and down there like a seasoned boxer and absorbed about half of the punch. Then she reversed the fighting tool and managed to knock the stick from Tug's hand with the end of the broom handle. All the while Tug was on the verge of crying, making sobbing noises under his loud breath. Oliver ordered Mandy Jo to go to his car and wait for him. The entire scene swelled with terror.

"You black bitch!" Tug yelled and hit Elma a third time. The blow grazed her temple, and again, she staggered and fell.

Oliver ran up and kicked Tug in the back with every bit of strength he could muster. Tug, barely affected, turned around and slugged Oliver. The punch only landed on his ear, but the slender hippie folded into the ground like a crumpled daffodil. Sirens began to echo through the concrete corridors. Then, Tug turned back to the prostrate Elma, grew red as a plum, and began to charge forth like a thunderous, angry tidal wave. Elma quickly picked up the stick she had knocked from the loathsome giant's hand and pointed it skyward. Just then, Phoenix made a break from the car window and ran right through Tug's charging feet, just as cats have a tendency to do, only he did it deliberately. The fast-moving big man tripped and plunged forth like a maniacal elephant, landing right onto the sharpened stick that Elma had held up from the ground. The stick pierced the left chamber of Tug's heart. The other end of the stick had pierced Elma's right side as all of the colossal man's weight had landed on it.

A loud grunt pierced the afternoon air and gave everyone a death chill. Elma laid there for a moment, then, with much labor, turned the big man over, the stick now protruding from his swollen chest. Everyone heaved with terror. Tug gurgled and his eyes bugged out of his head. His lips turned purple. His chest grew large like a 90-gallon garbage barrel. He bled inside quicker than the blood could escape the plugged hole in his left chest. The rest of his face now turned purple as he put his hand up to the wound, grabbing the stick as if to pull it out. But before he could yank on it, his arm collapsed to his side. He lay there gurgling and spitting up blood, while the sirens grew louder and louder. With one final death gasp, he expired on the spot where Elma had turned him over. He lay there like a fallen buffalo on an ancient Illinois prairie.

Elma, with great labor, pulled herself up from the ground. She yanked the stick from Tug's left chest, then she raised it high in the air, holding it with both hands, as if she would stab the colossal driver in the right chest. Suddenly, Oliver grabbed the frustrated women's arm and gripped it tightly, not allowing her to bring down the bloody stick for a second plunge.

"No!" yelled Oliver, "you'll get yourself into trouble!" Just then, the angry mother relaxed her grip on the stick and fell to her knees crying.

Jamelle tended to Elma, saying, "We all witnessed it ma'am. It was complete self-defense."

The once shiny Ghant! button on Tug's shirt was now smeared with blood, so that the face of the hate-peddler, Wackersham, was indiscernible.

One cop car after another whipped into the lot. The saga had turned to a new page.

AFTERMATH

"Oh Oliver," Mandy Jo exclaimed, "You were right all along! He was a monster!" Oliver comforted his mother and decided not to pressure her with "I-told-you-so's." Phoenix, who shared hero status with Elma, brushed against Oliver's leg, as if to indicate "everything is gonna be OK."

Soon, two ambulances carried Elma and Melanie to the hospital. Melanie ended up in the psyche ward for severe shock and depression.

Talking to Melanie, the cops quickly determined that the big man with a hole in his chest was the assailant. And, of course, everyone corroborated the story that Elma had only defended herself while trying to drive the monster off of the motel premises.

Upon searching the motel room, the cops found some long-nose pliers but not much else. They took fingerprints and swabbed some areas for DNA. When the forensics team took over, Detective Dave Allen left the room and pressed the button next to the elevator, which was only two doors down from room 209. But just as soon as the elevator doors opened, he noticed an oddity: two pointed sticks with one end of each embedded in the Styrofoam base of a fake house plant just next to the elevator. Suddenly, the notion that the sticks were familiar hit him like a power puncher's solid left hook. Then he realized that the attacker had put them there, and that he was really no victim at all, but he was instead the wanted predator, the Illinois Eye Digger!

"That sonofabitch," mused Detective Allen, "he was going to post that poor lady's eyeballs for everyone in the motel to see!" Again, the sticks pointed heavenward like a pair of unattached goal posts.

Detective Dave Allen's discovery was both chilling and revelatory. The pointed sticks, embedded in the fake house plant's base, confirmed the suspicions he had about the attacker. The realization that Tug was not a random assailant but the notorious Illinois Eye Digger sent a shiver down his spine. The pattern of the sticks—clearly intended to evoke a perverse symbolism—was unmistakable.

As the police continued their investigation, the connection between the sticks and the suspect became clearer. The quiver full of sharpened sticks found in the truck cab was a grim testament to Tug's horrifying intentions. The detectives knew

they were dealing with a deeply disturbed individual whose actions were driven by a twisted sense of brutality.

The interviews conducted with witnesses revealed a complex picture of the events. Melanie, still shaken, recounted her terrifying encounter with Tug, describing his attack with chilling detail. Elma's defense of herself was corroborated by multiple accounts, and her bravery in the face of such danger was evident.

Mandy Jo, despite her initial shock, managed to provide a clear account of her own experiences, convincing the police that she had been unwittingly involved. Her testimony, though confused at times, was consistent with the broader narrative of the incident.

The forensics team worked diligently, analyzing the DNA and fingerprints collected from the motel room and Tug's truck. The evidence began to paint a grim but precise picture of Tug's guilt. As the night wore on, the interviews and investigations slowly pieced together the sequence of events, building a strong case against the Illinois Eye Digger.

With the evidence mounting and the connections clear, the authorities prepared for the next steps. The case against Tug was solidifying, and it was only a matter of time before the full extent of his crimes would be revealed.

Elma required a surgery on her nose, and a bit of sewing up of her intestines, but she recovered well. Melanie Goodall would soon develop Post Traumatic Stress Disorder, though she had no obvious physical injuries aside from slight abrasions on her throat and left wrist and a sore ankle from propping open the motel room door. The motel staff eventually cleaned up the mess, mostly in the parking lot, and the cops impounded Tug's rig. Interviews with everyone involved went on into the dreary morning.

In front of the Blandon Police Headquarters, the public fountain, with the colors of the rainbow drenching its water, the effect of a circle of colored lights, glowed brilliantly in the solemn night.

They would all soon learn, during the police-station interviews, that Tug had a wife and six children, four of whom were adults. The couple had been separated for some six months and Tug had his own apartment.

Only a week after the cease in Tug's terror, Joy, his besieged wife, began to sell his Matchbox Cars on Ebay. And when cleaning out her closet, she had discovered a bag of toenail trophies, which Tug had secreted there while making a child-support payment, and which she promptly turned over to the cops. But the cops had already questioned Tug in the past and recognized the quiver full of double-sharpened sticks they found in the cab of Tug's truck, so they pretty much knew that Tug was the serial killer. Those cops checked Tug's DNA against the DNA they had found at some of the murder scenes, and to everyone's satisfaction, got a match. Tug, they then knew beyond all doubt, was the Illinois Eye Digger. A wave of shock, followed by relief, swept over the population when publicly announced.

ACCOLADES

When Elma got out of the hospital, she was treated like a hero wherever she went. The Mayor's Office of Blandon awarded her for her bravery, and *The Plant Rag* named her Person of the Year. Although the incident cast a shadow over the independent motel industry in Illinois and caused some financial strain for Sparky's Paradise Inn, the motel's management and employees showered Elma with praise. They provided her with snacks and all the little perks that come with being a hero in a mid-sized Midwest city. The support from the community and her workplace helped her feel valued and appreciated, offering a sense of closure and validation after her harrowing experience. Elma's heroic conquering of the Illinois

Eye Digger even elicited a few job offers, though nothing that paid very well.

For now, she would remain a loyal employee of Sparky's and bask in the attention that a few news articles brought her. So, the west side of town remained proud of their own Elma, and the hard-working motel maid breathed a tad easier when the excitement melted away and things turned back to normal.

Meanwhile, Tyrel too enjoyed some praise at school, and for a while was the star of his band. Even one of the bullies who tried to make him wear the Make America White Again cap congratulated him for being the son of a hero.

TURBULENT WATERS

On the East side of town, especially in the Goodall Mansion, the quietude ranked conspicuous. The lascivious prowling of the All-American, church-going business citizen, Melanie Goodall, gave impetus to the gory and bizarre incident, yet nary a peep of her involvement in the scandal passed through the innocent lips of the Blandon-Average public. That is because a couple of reporters from *The Plant Rag* and a certain cop in charge of the Public Relations Department at City Hall all attended the same Spongez church that The Two Mels attended, and a special agreement did not allow the leak into the public arena. So eerily did the silence prevail that Melanie carried on her personal and business affairs entirely unscathed.

But behind the hand-carved mahogany doors and stained-glass windows of the Goodall Mansion, Melvin and Melanie's once pristine relationship navigated through some rough waters. Despite the turmoil, the savvy couple managed to maintain their glittering, happy-family, toothpaste-commercial smiles for all the world to see.

THREE WEEKS LATER

Chicago Police Department, Homicide Division, Interview Room. The cops had summoned Tug's mother, Alice McRae, down to headquarters.

"Mrs. McRae, this is Detective Spalding and I'm Detective Hurley," said a wiry middle-aged woman with dark wavy hair and the slight appearance of a mustache. Tug's mother shook hands with the pair.

"State your full name please," said Detective Hurley.

"Alice M. McRae," said the now trembling woman.

"Was the late Douglas McRae, otherwise known as 'Tug,' your son?"

"Yes, he was."

"And where are you employed, Mrs. McRae?"

Alice shed a tear and answered almost inaudibly, "At the Chicago Helping Hand Organization. I work part-time as an aid and do some volunteer work as well."

Detective Spalding, a young man with dark hair and a very business-like demeanor, asked, "What kind of relationship did you have with your son, Mrs. McRae?"

"We were close later in life; not so much early on," Alice McRae began to weep.

"Is it true you supplied your son with phone numbers of prostitutes?" asked Detective Hurley.

"Well…yes, I did, but—"

"How did you acquire these numbers?"

"Like I said, I was an aid at CHHO…the Prostitution Outreach Society leg of the non-profit…organization," Alice sobbed.

"We…worked on a hotline number for those…sex workers in distress." Alice's weeping grew strong as she paused a moment. "We…also did intake…and furnished sleeping quarters…for the homeless prostitutes."

Detective Spalding injected himself abruptly, "Is it true, Mrs. McRae, that you gave out these numbers with the knowledge that your son, Douglas McRae, would murder these women?"

"Oh no, no. That's not true, sir." She paused again and wiped her tears with a napkin from a stack on the table.

"Then why do we have text messages recovered through Doug, or 'Tuggy,' as you called him—from his cellphone—indicating that you did, indeed, know of the girls' fate?"

"I...."

"Messages like this one, Mrs. McRae: 'Tuggy, I have a new number for you. This one's a real loose whore. Take care of her, son.'"

"I...." Alice openly bawled as she did at Tug's funeral.

"And this one," barked Detective Hurley, "Give this bitch the full treatment. She's a no-good complainer. A whiny wench. Give her the spike treatment, son!"

"What was the 'spike treatment,' Mrs. McRae?" yelled Detective Spalding. "The placing of eyeballs on sticks?"

"You may as well give yourself up, Mrs. McRae," ordered Detective Hurley. The tiny hairs above her lip seemed to dance merrily with anticipation. "We have ample evidence that you have committed conspiracy to murder!"

"It's to your benefit to explain your side of the story, unless you'll be satisfied with the death penalty!" hollered Detective Spalding.

"OK. I knew." With that admission Alice McRae seemed to calm down a bit, almost in relief.

"You knew what, Mrs. McRae?" asked Spalding, he too, a bit calmer.

"I knew that Tug would kill them," Alice McRae sobbed. "He was so neglected and abused as a child. I felt I had to make up for it. His father beat him tirelessly. I didn't give him enough attention. He was bullied in grade school, and when I first found out that he had murdered a girl—he would tell me anything—at a motel, I was going to turn him in, I swear. But…but he threatened me. And before I knew it, I was helping him with his evil deeds because I felt so sorry for him."

"But you didn't feel sorry for those poor women, did you, Mrs. McRae?" said Detective Hurley. "Or the children they left behind."

"Mrs. McRae, for aiding and abetting your son in these cold, callous acts—in this sociopathic madness," said Detective Spalding, "you are under arrest for conspiracy to commit murder."

Alice McRae was convicted and received 25 years in a federal penitentiary for her crime.

Melvin Goodall's part in setting up his wife's date at Sparky's Paradise Inn was never discovered by the cops or anyone else. But it was all just an innocent effort to please Melanie.

And here, the saga did not end the sordid affairs of the Tug McRae family, since the wife, Joy McRae's own children had abandoned her three years before, partly on account of her blind and brazen support for the racist Wackersham and partly on account of her refusal to believe that Tug was an animal torturer. The kids had spent immeasurable energy trying to dodge those knowledgeable about the family history. Now, the children had to deal with the ultimate embarrassment of being related to a serial killer. And so, through Tug's phone records and some notes between Tug and his mother, the cops realized that the mother had been funneling Tug the phone numbers of the prostitutes all along with the knowledge that they would soon die. Yet, no proof existed that Tug's spouse, Joy McRae, knew anything about the murders, nor did the cops think that was the case. But now, at least, the healing could begin.

WINTER BARRELS IN

A tremendous snowstorm had hammered Central Illinois. Now the wind and cold had enveloped Springfield and the place looked like one big ice sheet. Oliver and his friends sat in Ray's Roundup Restaurant sipping coffee and hot cocoa.

Oliver was due for a spiel, and boy, did he deliver it: "The damage done to America's reputation by not prosecuting Schmidt or Wackersham is far greater than the damage done by the insurrections they orchestrated. But this is the way the protectors of legacy want it. We have two complete misfits who tried to overthrow our democracy and we're all expected to act like manikins, with no feeling. I mean, personally, my trust in the American Justice System has been vanquished. Via time and the trickle effect they have managed to mitigate the severity of these fiendish acts. The people in charge of preserving America's legacy are charlatans!"

Oliver continued, "Sociologists and psychologists will toil for decades trying to rationalize the misguided veneration for these frauds. They will spend countless hours exploring and dissecting the population's willingness to coddle and pamper these putrid villains and lower themselves into abysmal subservience."

The waitress stopped by to give coffee refills. Oliver buzzed like a doorbell. Since nobody objected, he went on, "Maybe the world needs people who could blindly go about their lives as if nothing is wrong. Maybe I'm the problem. Maybe we need to just let the government operate as it sees fit and not say anything about it."

"Now," protested Jamelle, "you know that's not true, Oliver. Our forefathers noted that we should question our leaders."

"Maybe I should content myself by imitating the sniveling patsies in the Librhoid Party, who walk around in silence while the devious plutocrats dismantle our democracy. Or who whine about everything but do nothing."

"Now stop!" ordered Jamelle. "What would Lisa say? You questioning yourself like this...."

"Sorry."

"Lisa would not tolerate you giving up," Jamelle added.

"I know," assured Oliver. "You're right. Lisa was a strong young woman. She would have chased the chance to change the world for the better. She *did* change the world." Oliver paused and took a sip of his black coffee. "There are a lot of strong women in today's world. One thing they're going to have to give up, though, is the Gorebingerz religion. If they ever plan to be the true equal of the male species, they'll have to turn their backs on the Gorebingerz. That's because the Gorebingerz faith, like so many other religions, is predicated on the rule of man."

THREE YEARS LATER
BONKERS!

Several years of Wackersham had exacted a toll on weary Americans. The polls for the 2032 election looked very bleak for the aspiring tyrant. He grew hyper and irritable. He cursed his audiences; he demanded the masses to recommit themselves to the cause. He belittled reporters and throttled the government, slobbering and spitting like an over-excited dog as he raved on into the awkward nights. Finally, Wackersham had gone berserk. Even some in his own party were at a loss as to what to do with him. They had sunk their wretched claws in too deeply and now found themselves unable to retract them gracefully. The future of the entire movement to "rescue" America—essentially, to Make America White Again—depended on this foul-mouthed madman. His advocates would appear as a clan of blundering misfits if they attempted to back out of the slimy pit they had dug for themselves. But they also looked like misfits for doing nothing. So, they dithered and wrung their hands as their wounded image dragged on. Never a gloomier picture had shown on the screen of human destiny. And America laughed as it cried, the azure skies above it turning feces-brown and yucky yellow and filling with sludge-laden thunderheads, ready to pour their poison contents over the whole miserable country. And just then, before the ugly clouds could burst and flood the countryside with their ordure, the fatigued populace, up to its neck in despondency, voted him out of office. What should have been a landslide victory was only a narrow win, but a win it was. And the world, up to this time a nervous ball of worry, did not exactly rejoice, but simply staggered warily back to its corner and sat down, too tired and freaked out to celebrate. But the aging hellraiser and his bloated idea of himself and his goal of ruling like a king would finally shrink away and leave society to recover from its illness. For now, anyway, the Conservaprick Party lie in ruins.

"I mean I never cared for Conservapricks," moaned Oliver, "but this particular bunch has evolved into one grotesque criminal empire. That's right, the Conservaprick Party is now the Criminal Party."

"I agree," noted Jamelle. "Guys like 'Smug Tug' have a future with these underworld assholes in the Conservaprick ranks. But, for now, we are rid of them."

"But what if they come back with someone even worse than Wackersham?" fretted Oliver. "I mean, no one ever thought they could find someone worse than Oscar K. Schmidt, but they did when they elected Wackersham. So, who says they won't come up with someone even worse than Wackersham?"

"That's a future date I'll have to see to believe," admitted Jamelle. "What lies beneath the bottom, we cannot know at this point."

With the elimination of Douglas "Tug" McRae Springfield, Blandon-Average and the State of Illinois could rest easy. And now, with the disposal of Wackersham, the country—and perhaps the entire planet—could exhale one triumphant breath. At least the sane half. "Take a moment and relish the view," said Oliver Rhodes to his friends, "but make the break a short one. Behind the now tired cries of 'election fraud,' the reactionaries are toiling feverishly in their search for the next sinister, childish Conservaprick rogue to take the podium."

THE DEMISE OF JOY MCRAE

Oliver went on to earn an Associate Degree in Architecture. Elma found a job as a Computer Operator. True, it was not the programming position she had coveted, but it paid much better than her motel-maid position at Sparky's. Tyrel, after getting caught smoking pot and made to quit the band, was preparing for college. Mandy Jo never put her trust in another internet friend. The two Mels remained together but under a curtain of stress. They did not want to disappoint the church nor blemish their standing in the community with a divorce.

Joy McRae, the once lovely wife of Tug, struggled furiously with the revolting story that her husband was a torturer and serial killer, something she could no longer deny. Her hairy partner had exterminated and mutilated undeserving women. The shame of it all mummified her socially and ushered in an insurmountable degree of pain and angst. The more she squirmed in the heavy mud, the deeper she sank, until the gooey mixture stuck to her limbs like heated marshmallow. She wallowed in the muck of social pariah until her one and only friend urged her to move away, at which time she sold her condominium in Wheeling and scurried down to Oswego, Illinois. There she buried herself in political rallies for Ghant Wackersham, met new internet friends, and temporarily quelled the agony and mortification she had suffered since the day Tug died and the police informed her that she was the widow of a notorious serial killer. She traveled to Wackersham rallies in Charleston, South Carolina, Dallas, Texas, and Wichita, Kansas. She viciously unfriended anyone on Spacecrook who dared not cherish the President, for that was the one and only thing left that she had in common with her late husband: the love of Wackersham.

She joined the white supremacist paramilitary group The Frontier Confederates and made jokes with The Oaf Weepers. She wrote fervent racist papers and sent them to any organization willing to listen to her rants. For three and a half turbulent years, she battled "lost" liberals and torched the Librhoid Party. She couldn't let go and complained to anyone who would listen at the grocery store. Her psychologist told her she was crazy and needed psychiatric help and medication. The shock of Wackersham losing his re-election bid finally pushed her into psychotic episodes of anger and protest. Enticed by Wackersham and the beckoning of The Frontier Confederates, she participated in the insurrection at The Capitol on Inauguration Day, January 20, 2032. After the riot, she was arrested and charged with beating someone senseless with a Ghant! sign. The person later died, leading to a second-degree murder charge. For eternity, she would languish among the concrete and steel bars of the Federal Correction Institution Pekin.

Even in prison, she continued to sling accusations and racial epithets at liberal-thinking enemies. She devoted herself to condemning every Librhoid publication and praising far-right provocateurs. She cursed as if in a corner bar full of construction workers and blasted cyberspace with her wrath, targeting message-board liberals. Her relentless anger earned her awards from The Oaf Weepers and other far-right-wing organizations.

Then, in protest of her incarceration and the second life sentence she received for killing a liberal do-gooder in prison with a sharpened toothbrush handle, she hung herself with her own underwear, departing like a proud Conservaprick Queen.

Thus, the so-called "family morals" party was literally destroyed by perversity and fervid right-wing insanity. Oliver Rhodes had surmised: "As the world grows more complex, people become freakier and freakier, until fanaticism, paranoia, and racism permeate the social tapestry of America." Oliver also finally revealed what was inscribed on those secret chamber pots exhumed from the infamous South Chicago landfill by a mysterious Allcon prophet.

With four short words, the secrets of the universe were revealed:

Empty me at sunrise.

And the invention of the toilet, as we by now know, had displaced permanently the stinky chamber pot. And from there, life rambled into the 20th and 21st centuries.

With that enormous discovery of the chamber-pot writings, Oliver urged everyone to reflect on the miserable days of Ghant! The moral of the story, according to Oliver:

"Do not let them forget who they brought into our house."

Finally, The announcement in 2036 of the Two Mels' political hero, Ghant Wackersham, to run again held the two wealthy Christian elitists together as if they had been bonded by mortar. Meanwhile, one day while dining with his new girlfriend, Anna Washington, Oliver wrote on a napkin: "I'm the hippie of the 21st century. But this time we'll do it right. No hard drugs and no loose sex. And no dropping out like they did in the 60s and 70s. We'll go right after them Conservapricks and make this a more responsible planet, a planet where elite capitalists no longer rule, even if we have to dump the Librhoid Party to do it."

APPENDIX A

OLIVER'S REJECTED RECITAL IN PUBLIC SPEAKING CLASS (THE INSTRUCTOR WOULD NOT ALLOW HIM TO READ IT.)

To vote for a skunk just because it advertises lower taxes is a bit inglorious. To vote for a skunk because it hints at a shift back toward white male supremacy is an intolerable and egregious undertaking. And to vote for a skunk because you think he or she might provide a springboard to The Rapture is astonishingly lame and sinister.

Wackersham's image as the white darling of conservatism, the savior of American exceptionalism, tosses a bleak shadow over not only the concept of democracy but the whole of humanity. As the ratio of darker-skinned people to the total population increases, desperation on the part of ultra-conservatives grows at a debilitating rate.

The delusion of doom that white supremacists experience drives erratic and aggressive behavior, which in turn leads to violent measures aimed at preventing or eliminating the possibility of a white minority. We are living in precarious times that resemble the turbulence of the pre-Civil War era. America might be on the brink of significant change. One possibility is a second, guerrilla-type Civil War without clear dividing lines like north and south; another, though less likely, is a new understanding of human differences and a healing of spirit.

The problem lies in the theory that once fascism infects the human psyche, it continues to grow and fester into an indomitable force. When this dangerous seed spreads among a group of minds, it poses a severe threat to society. Pockets of fascism have emerged in the form of far-right militias and hate groups scattered across the country. These groups have shown a tendency to unite and wreak havoc, as evidenced by their actions at the Capitol on January 20, 2032. The attack resulted in over 1,300 American deaths, nearly 75,000 injuries, and approximately $3 billion in damages.

Is the American government taking effective steps to counter their attempts to impose a white America through violent outbursts and collective actions? Is their backward march so infectious that the fringe elements will soon be joined by the more mainstream elements?

These questions will likely be answered in the next few years. Meanwhile, the teetering continues.

So, one must ask her- or himself: Have you ever witnessed a fascist-leaning inclination that shrinks? Once planted, the tree usually grows. How wide and high it grows is a question for the ages.

APPENDIX B

OLIVER'S STREET CORNER INTERVIEWS

Three impeachment proceedings and sixty-four recommended charges to the Department of Justice, as well as fourteen rape charges, had not dampened the infatuation with Wackersham. His crude base still adored their man, worshiped him, in fact.

Oliver had to know at what point, if any, Wackersham's followers would turn on him. So, one gloomy day, he grabbed his old cassette tape recorder and went to the corner of 5th Avenue and Jefferson Street in downtown Springfield and conducted interviews with the public.

"I am trying to discern at what point you would remove your support for Ghant Wackersham." asked the curious interviewer. "Would you turn your back on Wackersham if he:

(A) stole from your neighbor

(B) stole from a friend

(C) stole from a family member

(D) stole from you

(E) none of the above.If the interviewee answered "E," he or she would graduate to the next set of questions.Would you turn your back on Wackersham if he:

(A) defecated on your lawn

(B) defecated on your living room floor

(C) defecated on your lap

(D) defecated in your face

(E) none of the above.

If the interviewee also answered "E" to this last inquiry, he or she would graduate to the exceptional status of "Goner" and also to an Honorary Citizen of The Wackersham Worshipers' Committee, a committee that practices in the art of feet kissing, toe licking and rump petting.

Of course, hardly anyone wanted to answer the second question. Those who did respond often became violent. Oliver, seeking to provoke more shock value, substituted the word "defecated" with "shit." As a result, he endured numerous insults, two shoves, and one punch to the jaw. Did he back down? No. Oliver was determined to push boundaries, even going so far as to replace "defecated in your face" with "shit in your mouth." The first person he used this on seized his tape player and smashed it on the sidewalk. Nonetheless, Oliver managed to recover the tape.

In closing the recording, Oliver used another tape machine to make his point about the nature of the common mouth, which he felt epitomized Wackersham: "The mouth is laden with bacteria—the dirtiest of holes. It serves as a conduit for the brain to transmit unfiltered stupidity into the air. A good motto to follow is this: Politicians by mouth; doers by action."

APPENDIX C

OLIVER'S POLEMIC AGAINST A WAYWARD RELIGIOUS STATE

Oliver Rhodes penned an opinion piece for *The Harsh Awakening*, an underground news source both in print form and on the web. He pulled out a clipping of the 2024 editorial with the intention of updating his handful of readers here in 2032.

Original Article: June 12, 2024

Snoring Through Madness

In the cradle of conflict, Quasar had gradually installed an extremist, far-right regime, and now, while waiting to embark on a new-age thrust to seize power and "dilate" the Thronez' burgeoning empire, they secretly coiled like a snake ready to pounce on its prey. America just sat there during the entire mutation and pretended that nothing had happened.

Finally, the time arrived when a minority of Pulsarian extremists, exhausted by endless oppression, segregation, and discrimination, launched a brutal attack on a group of concertgoers, killing about 200 innocent Thronez. In response, a vengeful Quasar launched a disproportionate retaliation, wreaking havoc on Pulsar villages and indiscriminately mutilating thousands of inhabitants. Western media largely downplayed the violence, referring to it as a war rather than a one-sided massacre. Lesser-known news sources, however, reported that 14,000 Pulsarian children had been killed before half the year had even passed. Despite the fundamentalist extremists taking over the Quasar government and orchestrating the brutal assault on

Pulsar, America foolishly supported its old ally, Quasar. And the Librhoid Party allowed this massacre to take place without doing a thing to prevent it or even speak out against it. In fact, they actually funded the massacre. With America's prior illegal blitz on Irad and its tacit support for Quasar's genocide in Pulsar, the nation now finds itself in a precarious position on the global stage. The apartheid state of Quasar had clearly committed genocide, and America had stood by, with some of its more extreme elements even rallying in support of the violence, hoping to impose their own grimy right-wing agenda.

Amid this dark backdrop, a beacon of resistance has emerged. American college students have begun to protest the relentless bombing of Pulsar by Quasar's military forces. This movement echoes the protests of the 1970s, when hippies rallied against the Vietnam War. Despite the drug use and sexual excesses of that era, those protests ultimately contributed to ending a war. Now, after decades of crack- and meth-fueled violence, the spirit of the hippie is re-emerging in the form of a new generation fighting for justice.

In closing, let us harbor no hatred toward the Thronez but only disdain for the fanatical government that has materialized.

Update: June 12, 2032

After six years of unjust offensives, the Quasars have annexed new lands by chasing off or exterminating the native population. It reminds one of the way a young America vanquished and pushed out the American Indian. With a callous military built up via American dollars, Quasar, in 2032, now poses a threat to humanity. Though Iran still haunts the Thronez' State, Quasar has stockpiled tons of weaponry. They own a nuclear arsenal that rivals that of Russia and America. They decimated the idea of a two-state solution and now have their eyes on further expanding their empire. Meanwhile, America sips lemonade and falls asleep.

APPENDIX D

OLIVER'S FINAL HARANGUE: THE CAPITALIST SHIT SHOW

"Rock music grates on my nerves anymore," said Oliver to his friend, Jamelle. "I'm in the process of switching to jazz. I'm so sick of arena rock, rock-ballad clichés, rock music in commercials and radio overplay.

"I've had it with rock solo artists. Where has the fucking band gone?"

"Yeah," agreed Jamelle, "we're either in a real dead zone or rock is washed up forever."

Both young men sipped at their colas while the radio at Ray's Roundup Restaurant played an old Talking Heads song. The place lacked the old buzz of Oliver's college days, but it still served as one of the coolest hangouts in Springfield.

"Oh," said Jamelle, "I almost forgot. I looked into the mistreatment of the Pulsarians at the hands of Quasar. I found that there is some truth about the oppression thing."

"Well," admitted Oliver, "you're probably the first person out of everyone I've ever talked to who actually looked into it."

But we still need to stress that we offer no safe place for those who want to steer hatred toward the Thronez, especially American Thronez. There's no place for that."

"Hey brother," assured Jamelle, "I'm with you."

"Some people," noted Oliver, "do not like Thronez because they are so good with money. I mean, you know Americans.

They've got to have everything now. They do not care for holding onto a dollar bill. But, because the average Thronez chooses to do so, the average earthling harbors a terrible envy and an unfounded resentment of this patient behavior. Later on, 'cause they pissed away all of their money…that is to say, when they are old, broke and hungry, that envy transforms into hatred. Stupid Americans should, instead, take a lesson from the frugal Thronez. SAVE YOUR MONEY!"

"What about Wackersham?" asked Jamelle. "Have you heard the latest?"

"Oh," replied Oliver, "you mean about the fourteen women who have come forward with rape charges? Yeah, I heard." Oliver drank the last bit of his cola. "What about the four charities he ripped off? You heard that?"

"Oh, it's four now?" asked Jamelle. "The last I heard it was two. You know, it's just a never-ending cycle of filth with that guy," laughed Jamelle. "The crimes keep comin' and they still love him. In fact, the more crimes he's charged with, the more the perverse adulation with him flowers."

"I couldn't have said it better," Oliver said. "You know, I'm afraid to talk to my old friends… in case they are Wackersham fans."

"Do you think America can heal from this gigantic, gaping wound?" asked Jamelle.

"Well, the Diagnostic and Statistical Manual of Mental Disorders, otherwise known as the DSM, may not list this kind of mass depravity," Oliver responded. "It has just never occurred before that I know of. I mean, history is full of group trends. Just look at the Beatles' popularity—hordes of screaming girls. But I don't know of a mass attraction to something as raunchy as a Wackersham."

This remains a mystery of mammoth proportions. Scientists surely have no answer to this phenomenon of aggregate idiocy. Whether America can heal from this glob of twisted profusion—this sick adoration for something of such putridity is the great question of our time."

"Ever thought about leaving America?" queried Jamelle.

"Well, yeah, but I'm stickin' it out. Wackersham's finally gone. Quasar has lost its good reputation. Hell, even Tug McRae has expired. I've got an internship with a good architectural firm now and I'm here to stay."

"Me too," added Jamelle.

"You know," said Oliver, "I've always wondered what it would be like if all of the people around the world suddenly figured it out that all religion is a hoax that nothing happens after death but utter darkness.

"What kind of horrific panic would overwhelm us?" Oliver asked.

"Now there's where you and I disagree," Jamelle retorted, giving Oliver a friendly tap on the upper arm. "And the capitalists?" Jamelle continued. "What are your latest thoughts... now that you are one of them?"

"Hey," replied Oliver, "I'm just doing what I have to do to survive. I ain't no capitalist. I mean, what have the industrialists brought us? Filthy rivers, tainted soil, and putrid air. And really dumb people. Forget their sale barns, bargain bins, and wall-to-wall ads. They and their goddamn 'commerce' can stick their dicks in the wall for all I care. They've sucked America dry, and

I'm sure not going to celebrate it. I mean, to hell with their refinance options and their everlasting, 365-day-a-year overlapping holiday seasons."

Their mothers should have strangled them with their own neckties."

"That's my boy," said Jamelle with a wink. "Just checkin' to see if you still had that old spark."

"What I want to know," added Oliver, "is when will they have a 'Beat Your Boss Day?'"

The pair laughed as the dim lights of Ray's Roundup Restaurant cast an easy shadow on the multitudinous feet tapping to some old, overplayed rock tune that blared on the radio. Life wears on, thought Oliver.

APPENDIX E

THE SINUOUS SINS OF SATAN

Yes, yes, yes, the foul fiend, Oscar K. Schmidt, was finally convicted of multiple felonies, but how long will they stick? If they somehow made it past the appeals process and all the way up to the Supreme Court, the buddies Schmidt and Wackersham installed will strip him of the "felony" label quicker than a two-bit gigolo will strip off his trousers for a shriveled, old widow. And should his conviction somehow stand, the sitting President will pardon him before leaving office, if not sooner. Now then, should the greatest miracle ever known to the human race transpire, and the grifter of time immemorial should retain his felonious status, he will be patted on the rump and granted probation, with all of his sycophants waiting in line to slobber all over his vindictive countenance like a pack of eager puppies. And the Protectors of Legacy will be toiling arduously all summer long to downplay his criminality and recast his image.

From any angle we view it, *Reputation America*, that righteous, old stalwart, has received a vigorous thrashing, even if the countless throngs of deviants can never comprehend it, for, no matter the transgression, no matter the folly, no matter the error, the purveyors of grim depravity will embrace him like a cockroach on a cornflake. Exhibition in whoremastery? All men do that! Multiple impeachments? He was railroaded. Multiple felonies? He was a victim of politicalization. And the Conservaprick shit wagon rolls on and on….

America has grown filthy because of it.

APPENDIX F

SELLING HIMSELF FROM A CELL

On May 16, 2034, Alfred J. Crumplehorn announced from a Louisiana penitentiary jail cell his candidacy for President of the United States of America in the 2036 election. Fans of the new Conservaprick Champion took to immediate celebration. Crumplehorn boasted of his past support of both Schmidt and Wackersham. In fact, he served as a Cabinet Member during Wackersham's term of office. The Conservaprick Party, now commonly known as "The Criminal Party," fully embraced the contemptible scuzzbag. The scoundrel was banking on his release at his very first parole hearing in January, 2035. His 24-year sentence for bigamy, kidnapping, racial hate crimes, and pedophilia would not deter this otherwise "wholesome" right-wing candidate from seeking office and starting anew in his cringeworthy life. And, not more than twelve hours after his announcement, Crumplehorn-loving Conservapricks were busy making Alfred! signs. Country diners already buzzed with the exciting news. Conservative church crowds rushed to brunches to discuss the topic. And, in Illinois, it was like a new hand from heaven had reached down to re-bless the Pods of Bubbledumb. Indeed, new Pods were avidly hatching in the cornfields of Blandon-Average.

A Special Note from Your Author:

If a Pod ever wanders into your back yard:

Don't pet it.

Instead, flail it vigorously with a rug beater or similar device.

Perhaps you can scare it away.

But don't expect to knock any sense into it.

Remember, Pods are forever.

Milton Keynes UK
Ingram Content Group UK Ltd.
UKHW042306101024
449571UK00002B/10